AF585221

Jurassic World franchise © 2022 Universal City Studios LLC and Amblin Entertainment, Inc. Series © DreamWorks Animation LLC. All rights reserved.

Published by Scholastic Australia in 2022.

Scholastic Australia Pty Limited
PO Box 579 Gosford NSW 2250
ABN 11 000 614 577
www.scholastic.com.au

Part of the Scholastic Group
Sydney • Auckland • New York • Toronto • London • Mexico City
New Delhi • Hong Kong • Buenos Aires • Puerto Rico

All rights reserved. No part of this publication may be reproduced or transmitted in any form or by any means, electronic or mechanical, including photocopying, recording, storage in an information retrieval system, or otherwise, without the prior written permission of the publisher, unless specifically permitted under the Australian Copyright Act 1968 as amended.

ISBN 978-1-76112-464-8

Printed by McPherson's Printing Group, Maryborough, VIC.

Scholastic Australia's policy, in association with McPherson's Printing Group, is to use papers that are renewable and made efficiently with wood from responsibly managed sources, so as to minimise its environmental footprint.

10 9 8 7 6 5 4 3 2 1   22 23 24 25 26 / 2

The paper in this book is FSC® certified. FSC® promotes environmentally responsible, socially beneficial and economically viable management of the world's forests.

CAMP CRETACEOUS

VOLUME FOUR:
THE NOVEL

Adapted by Steve Behling
Cover illustrated by Patrick Spaziante

SCHOLASTIC
SYDNEY AUCKLAND NEW YORK TORONTO LONDON MEXICO CITY
NEW DELHI HONG KONG BUENOS AIRES PUERTO RICO

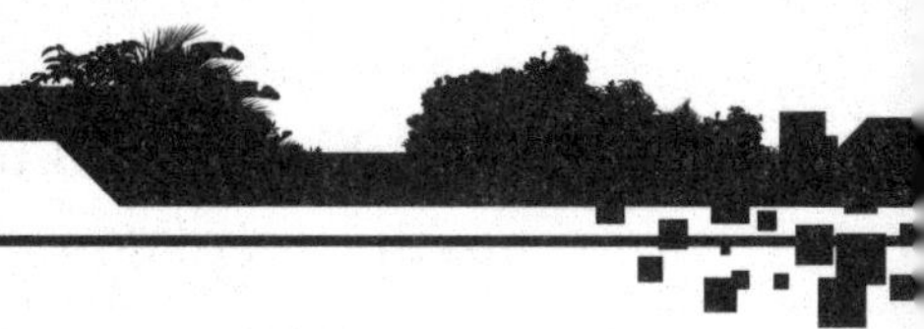

CHAPTER ONE

"Okay, so . . . *definitely* not Costa Rica," Brooklynn said.

After all those times they were nearly devoured by dinosaurs at Jurassic World, Darius and his friends had finally escaped Isla Nublar. Only hours before, helicopters had arrived when the kids first attempted their departure on a rickety yacht. But they weren't there on a rescue mission. They were part of a mercenary operation led by Dr. Henry Wu to retrieve important data from the island.

The kids took their chances with the mercenaries and got separated. Wu was after a laptop that contained his top-secret genetic research. Brooklynn grabbed the laptop, then gave it to Darius as she was captured by the mercenaries. An exchange was arranged—the laptop for Brooklynn. The kids saved Brooklynn and destroyed Wu's laptop. They fled in their boat, only to have it destroyed by a Mosasaurus. Darius nearly drowned.

Then they washed up on the shore of . . . wherever it was they were now.

They stood on a cliff that overlooked a desert landscape.

"Any idea where we are?" Brooklynn asked.

Darius began to pace. "There's gotta be a way to figure it out," he said. "The direction of the sun maybe? Or if we could . . . hmm. Maybe if we . . . How about . . ."

Sammy sat down next to Yasmina. Brooklynn followed suit, then Kenji.

"We just gotta assess the situation," Darius said, trying to sound hopeful.

"No food. No water. No shelter," Brooklynn grumbled. "No civilization, so . . ."

"Situation assessed," Yasmina finished. "We're doomed. Again." She flicked a pebble off the cliff to emphasize her point. Unsure what to do next, Darius sat down on the ground with his friends and rested his head in his hands.

"Oh, my sweet, frightened children," Ben said. "We didn't know how we were gonna survive on Nublar, and yet, we did. By sheer will, determination, and teamwork. Like Darius said, there aren't even dinosaurs here! Logically, this should be easier! So let's go out there and, ya know, survive!"

One by one, the kids rose to their feet. What Ben had said made sense!

Darius saw Brooklynn looking off into the distance.

"Look, over there," she said. "Something shiny!"

The kids jumped up and down, trying to catch a glimpse of what Brooklynn had spotted.

"Looks like the sun is glinting off of some sort of . . . metal thingy," Sammy said.

"Something metal probably means someone made it," Darius said.

Ben was already heading down the rocks. The group followed.

"This place is weird, right?" Darius replied. "It's like another planet or something."

Taking a step, Darius was surprised when his foot caught on something in the sand. He reached down and pulled out what looked like a rusted metal pole with something on the end.

"What is that?" Yasmina said.

"It looks like some sort of metal claw," Darius replied.

"Because dinosaurs weren't enough. Now we're washed up on some deserted island with weird, disembodied claws?" Yasmina moaned.

As the sun got higher in the sky, the endless walk across the island seemed all the more . . . endless. Then Sammy said, "Uh, guys?" She pointed at a huge dark cloud coming toward them.

"Seriously? A sandstorm?" Brooklynn groaned.

"Reminds me of those pesky rainstorms we used to outrun on Nublar," Ben said. "Except, ya know, with dirt. I bet we can outrun this thing, too!"

And with that, Ben sprinted off. Not knowing what else to do, the group followed, racing across the sand as fast as they could. The sandstorm blew ever closer, but the kids seemed to be keeping ahead of it. Maybe they really *could* outrun it!

Suddenly, the storm surged, enveloping the kids in darkness! They became separated.

"Hello?!" Darius called out.

"Where is everybody?" Kenji hollered. He bumped into Brooklynn! She grabbed Kenji's arm and held on tightly.

The sand continued to blow, but Darius thought it was letting up a little bit. He could see in front of him. And then he saw Ben, Yasmina, and Sammy.

"Wait!" Sammy said. "Where are Kenji and Brooklynn?"

"You okay?" Brooklynn asked.

She and Kenji had fallen through the sand, landing at the bottom of what appeared to be a cavern.

"Yeah, of course," Kenji said.

"What is this place?" Brooklynn asked.

They called for their friends, but no one answered.

"We're alone," Brooklynn said.

"We never should have tried to outrun that storm," Ben said. "What was I thinking?"

Darius felt bad for Ben, who was blaming himself. He took a step forward, then felt Yasmina pull him back. He looked down and saw a huge cavern that had been revealed by the sandstorm. One more step and he would have fallen in!

"Maybe they fell down there," Sammy said.

Darius squinted. "They're not there now . . . which means they survived. Now all we gotta do is find them."

"Do you hear that?" Brooklynn asked.

"Water pipes?" Kenji replied. "How could there be water pipes in here?"

They kept walking through the cavern. After a while, Brooklynn shouted, "There! I bet that's a way out!"

She scrambled up a wall of boulders as the sound of water rushing through pipes grew louder. Atop the boulders, Brooklynn saw light filtering through cracks.

Kenji was right behind her as they came to a plateau. Kenji gave her a boost, and she climbed up. Then she pulled Kenji up. He leaned against another rock, and suddenly, it gave way and light poured into the cavern. Kenji nearly fell over, and Brooklynn grinned and said "There. That wasn't so hard, was it?"

"Well, I do make everything look easy," Kenji replied.

The two looked at each other and smiled, then Brooklyn said, "Come on."

As night approached, Darius and his friends arrived at a wall of boulders. Ben ran over to the wall and searched the rocks.

"There's no way in," he said. "And we don't even know if they're in there."

Ben leaned against a boulder, then slid down to the ground. Placing his head in his hands, he said, "This is all my fault."

"Ben, it's okay," Darius said. "We just gotta figure out a way to move these rocks."

"No, ya don't!"

Darius turned his head, only to see Brooklynn and Kenji right behind them!

"You made it!" Ben said, beside himself.

"Yeah," Brooklynn said. "Strongman Kenji pushed an entire boulder out of the way."

“It was nothing,” Kenji replied, blushing a little. “Not a big deal.”

Darius tilted his head. “Wait, Kenji’s not taking credit for something cool he did?”

Changing the subject, Kenji said, “And, we’ve got more good news!”

Brooklynn smiled, gesturing for them to follow. She and Kenji led the group to a waterfall. Everyone leaned down to the pool beneath it, cupped their hands to gather water, and drank.

“The weird thing is, we heard water pipes in the cavern,” Kenji said. “Somebody *built* this.”

Everyone stopped drinking and looked at Kenji.

“But why?” Darius asked.

“And where are they now?” Yasmina said, her eyes darting back and forth.

“No idea,” Brooklynn replied. “But if we can find that shiny thing, maybe we’ll get some answers.”

They started walking and soon came to the top of a dune. There was just enough sun left for them to see a metallic glint.

“There it is!” Sammy whooped.

But when they moved in, all they saw was a shiny metal platform set into the sand.

“A metal rectangle?” Kenji said. “That’s all it was?”

Next to the rectangle, Brooklynn made an unpleasant discovery.

“There’s also these animal bones,” she said.

Not knowing what else to do, the group started a bonfire for warmth. Exhausted, they eventually fell asleep.

Ben's eyes popped open. He heard a slight rustle in the darkness. He began to breathe faster as his pulse quickened.

"What is it?" Yasmina whispered.

"Wake everyone up," Ben replied. "There's something out there." He picked up a stick and shoved the end into the bonfire, then raced to some shrubs nearby and used the stick to set them on fire, forming a wall.

"Let's go!" Ben said as his sleepy friends began to move.

They heard a growl.

"Run!" Ben ordered.

At once, the kids scattered away from the bonfire as a huge beast pounced!

"A saber-toothed tiger?!" Brooklynn said, amazed.

The beast was almost upon them—it was fast.

"We can't outrun it!" Darius said.

But Ben had an idea. He ran away from the group.

"Hey! Toothy!" he called out. "Easy meal, this way!"

Immediately, the sabertooth went for Ben.

Catching sight of the cavernous opening in the ground ahead, Ben ran to the edge and jumped down!

Unable to stop, the saber-toothed tiger skidded along the sand and tumbled into the cavern.

"We gotta help him!" Darius cried out.

Ben landed on the ground below with a thud, followed by the tiger. It appeared dazed, but Ben couldn't take his eyes off the animal. Ben backed around a corner and sprinted down the cavern.

"I'm going in," Kenji replied, and he dove in after Ben. The smaller boy heard the growl of the saber-toothed tiger not far behind him. He ran faster, trying to put more space between him and his pursuer. There came another loud growl, and when Ben looked back, he was face to face with the sabertooth!

Ben screamed, shutting his eyes as the beast roared. But as he slowly opened his eyes, he saw that the saber-toothed tiger had stopped short of him!

And then he saw Kenji standing behind the animal, pulling hard on its tail.

"Ben, get out of here!" Kenji yelled as the cat tried to get Kenji, swiping at him with its claws. Ben managed to get out of its way as it flung Kenji aside.

The animal pounced as Kenji rolled away, and it hit the cavern wall.

"Now what?" Ben wondered.

"I didn't have a plan beyond getting past the teeth!" Kenji said.

The saber-toothed tiger recovered quickly. The only way out was to climb. But there was no way the boys would be able to do that before the beast arrived.

Suddenly, a massive boulder fell from above, crashing to the ground behind the two boys, blocking the sabertooth! Ben and Kenji had no idea that their friends had pushed the giant rock, but regardless, they wasted no time scrambling out of the deadly hole.

With Kenji and Ben now safe, the kids resumed their desert trek. They broke into some singing to occupy the time, tossing a rock back and forth to decide whose turn it was to sing.

After Darius's turn, he threw the rock to Kenji. But he overthrew it, so Kenji ran to catch it. Before he could grab it, the rock hit an invisible barrier and fell to the sand. Kenji was moving fast and slammed into the barrier, too.

Brooklynn took a step forward and put a hand in front of her. The invisible barrier felt like a glass wall! She walked along the barrier with her hand extended. The glass wall kept on going.

There was the sound of a hydraulic mechanism—*pshhhht*—and an unseen door in the barrier opened! An eerie blue light poured from a corridor. The group stared at one another, utterly perplexed.

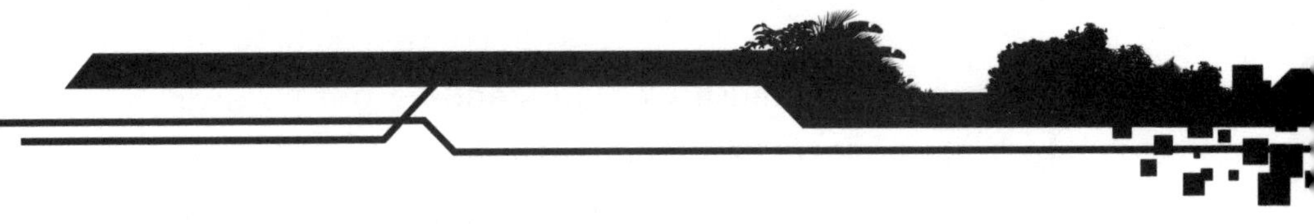

CHAPTER TWO

"Uh, remember how five seconds ago we were in a *desert*?"

Brooklynn stood in front of the open airlock door in awe. Ahead of her, she saw a lush forest with giant, looming trees. The landscape was as full of life as the desert was barren.

"Keep alert," Darius warned. "There could be more saber-toothed tigers or—"

But Darius was cut off by several loud booms, and the ground shook all around them. Darius's eyes grew wide. He knew that sound.

"T. rex!" Ben hissed.

Darius looked in horror as a towering T. rex headed right for them! The group sprinted into the forest, diving behind a huge tree. But the T. rex kept coming.

And then it ran right past them! The dinosaur ran to another, smaller T. rex. To Darius's surprise, the dinosaurs didn't fight. Instead, they nipped at each other.

Then he noticed a woman standing not far away. She had a tablet in her hand and appeared to be making notations. The woman watched as one T. rex smashed into a tree. She didn't even flinch!

The kids waved their arms, trying to catch the woman's attention—without drawing the attention of the huge carnivore. She looked over at the group, smiled, and waved, as if nothing was wrong. Then she turned her attention back to the T. rexes. A second later, the smile fell from the woman's face as if she had suddenly realized that something was wrong. She marched over to the kids.

"You're trespassing! What're you up to?" the woman said in a hushed voice. "Are you here to spy?"

That's when Darius finally realized that the dinosaurs weren't fighting. They were playing!

"Craniofacial biting!" Darius said as he watched the T. rexes.

"Uh . . . yes," the woman said. She turned serious. "Don't change the subject!"

"Lady, we don't wanna be here, either," Yasmina said. "We just wanna go home."

"Oh yeah," the woman said. "We'll see about that. Follow me."

Darius leaned out from behind the tree and saw the bigger T. rex looking at them. The dinosaur must have heard them talking! No one made a sound, and a moment later, the dinosaurs began playing once more as the kids followed the woman.

"You expect me to believe that children survived alone on Isla Nublar for six months?" the woman said in disbelief, after hearing their story.

They walked through a biome of sequoia trees, then into a clearing. Darius couldn't help staring at the woman. Something about her seemed familiar.

Behind them, a T. rex roared. The kids jumped as the woman stared at her tablet screen.

"Don't worry," she said. "They're almost tuckered out. They won't bother us."

"How could you know that?" Ben asked.

"It's kind of my thing," the woman said proudly. "Behavioral paleoneurobiologist, which is an extremely long way to say I study dinosaur brains. I'm Mae—"

"Turner!" Darius shouted. "That's it! You're Dr. Mae Turner!"

Dr. Turner nodded.

Darius looked like his head was going to explode as he shook her hand. "It's an honor to meet you. I read your book, *A Theoretical Emotional Journey with Theropods*!"

"Well," Kenji said with a sigh, "if you could just point us to a phone, we'll be on our way."

Dr. Turner stopped walking. "Yyyyyeah. Slight problem with that. This island is completely shut off the grid. No communications in or out."

"Are you kidding?!" Yasmina said.

Brooklynn pointed at the doctor's tablet. "You can't use that to call out?"

"Sorry. Closed-circuit. Mainly I use this to connect to a doodad in their brains, and—"

Dr. Turner showed the tablet to Brooklynn. There was an image of a dinosaur brain with different areas lighting up. Then she clutched the screen to her chest.

"Can't tell you, actually," she said. "Proprietary research."

"So there's no way home," Yasmina said, exhausted.

"Don't lose faith," Dr. Turner said as she held Yasmina's hand. "You can all rest up at my place until we figure out how to get you out of here."

"That sounds great," Darius said. "So the saber-toothed tiger and the T. rexes," Darius said as the group continued their walk through the trees. "Your bosses are making prehistoric creatures?"

"Some," Dr. Turner replied. "Although they got the T. rexes from Isla Sorna. Not that I should be telling you any of this."

"And the different landscapes?" Sammy asked, ignoring the doctor. "Why—"

"Hold up! Important announcement time!" Dr. Turner said, stopping in her tracks. She pointed at a valley nearby, and her voice took on a very serious tone. "Whatever you do, do *not* go down there. *Super*-dangerous."

Darius strained his neck, but it was impossible to see anything.

"All right," Dr. Turner said, bright and cheery once more. "Off we go!"

The kids wondered, Was there *really* something dangerous, or was Dr. Turner hiding something?

Dr. Turner took the kids up a long, winding path that led directly to a waterfall, and then walked beyond that, to a large cave. The area was divided into several spaces—a living area, a research section, and a kitchen.

"I'm gonna go whip up some sandwiches!" Dr. Turner said, heading for the kitchen.

Brooklynn looked at Kenji and started to search through Dr. Turner's stuff.

"What are you doing?" Darius demanded.

"We're not gonna just take her word for it there's no phone here," Brooklynn said.

"I guess it doesn't hurt to look around," he said uncomfortably.

Darius and Sammy explored the research area while Brooklynn dug through some filing cabinets.

"No phone," Darius said as he kept looking. "I think she's telling us the truth."

Then he noticed something on a board. There were

images of dinosaur brains, along with various notations like HUNGRY and TIRED.

"Whoa," Darius said. "She's matching their brain patterns to different behaviors!"

Sammy gasped, looking at a document in her hands. At the top of the page was a familiar logo.

"Mantah Corp.," Sammy said.

"Guess we know why this island is so secret," Ben replied.

"If Mae works for Mantah Corp., then we gotta get out of here," Brooklynn added.

Just then, Dr. Turner appeared behind them. "Who wants a sandwich?" she asked.

As the kids sat down and started eating their sandwiches, Dr. Turner left the group to get them something to drink.

"Let's check out that 'dangerous' area," Brooklynn suggested. "What if there's a phone or a way off the island and she's just trying to keep us away from it?"

Darius watched as Yasmina, Kenji, and Ben nodded together. "Okay," he said. "I'll keep her busy while you check it out."

"I'll stay, too," Sammy said. "Maybe we'll get some answers while we're at it."

Yasmina, Kenji, Ben, and Brooklynn quietly exited the cave. A moment later, Dr. Turner was back with a hot kettle.

"Where did everyone go?" she asked.

Sammy and Darius made a quick excuse about them needing showers and taking naps.

Darius looked at the readouts of dinosaur brains once again. "Wait a minute," he said. "I think I know what you're doing here. The brain patterns, the behaviors . . . You figured out how to tell what a dinosaur is . . . feeling?"

"Hypothetically," Dr. Turner said. "Mm-hmm!"

Yasmina, Kenji, Ben, and Brooklynn made it to the "superdangerous" area. Ben saw that the valley appeared to be littered with bones. In the center, he saw the edges of a metallic platform.

"Another metal rectangle," Ben said. "Like the one we saw in the desert."

"The bones . . . It's a feeding platform!" Brooklynn said.

"So, *hypothetically,* this is the coolest thing ever," Darius said, completely nerding out.

"I know!" Dr. Turner said, joining him. "We can anticipate their needs."

"So, *hypothetically*, what do your bosses plan to do with your research?" Sammy asked.

"I can't say," Dr. Turner replied. "Because I don't know. But I assume once this research facility is up and running, we'll just be making scientific breakthroughs left and right!"

Sammy could see that Dr. Turner really meant what she said.

"Did you hear that?" Brooklynn asked.

The group was heading back from the "super-dangerous" valley when they heard a rustle and ducked behind a boulder. They watched as the shrubs shook, and a second later, a Compsognathus appeared.

A large, four-legged robot entered the area. The robot scanned its surroundings with a green light that landed on the Compy.

"Unauthorized life-form detected," the robot intoned.

Electricity crackled as the robot blasted the Compy.

Brooklynn gasped, attracting the robot's attention. It scanned the vicinity and came closer.

An alarm went off in Dr. Turner's lab.

"'Unauthorized life-form detected in sector four,'" she said, checking her tablet. "'Elimination Protocol initiated.' That sounds extreme."

Sammy and Darius must have looked awful, because Dr. Turner said, "What is it?"

"Our friends are out there!" Darius blurted.

The robot came closer, scanning left and right. Kenji thought for sure the thing would find them.

Then he heard footsteps.

Kenji looked around the boulder and saw Dr. Turner standing right in front of the robot. The robot scanned her, and its red eye turned white.

"Dr. Mae Turner," the robot said evenly. "Authorized life-form. What can I do to assist you?"

"Never do *that* again, for starters!" the doctor said.

Darius and Sammy, still behind the tree, watched everything transpire.

"The metal claw from the desert—it was from one of these things!" Darius whispered.

With the danger gone, Kenji, Ben, Yasmina, and Brooklynn rejoined the group while Dr. Turner continued to distract the robot.

"Primary directive is to protect the ecostasis of the biome. Finishing patrol," the robot declared.

Then it took off, walking in the opposite direction of

the kids. Dr. Turner headed back to the group and said, "Thank goodness you're all okay."

"What was that thing?!" Brooklynn asked.

"One of the BRADs," Dr. Turner explained. "Bio-Robotic Assistance Droids. They care for the island, protect it if necessary. But I had no idea *that's* how they do it! We have to get you back to the cave. They're not allowed in there. It'll be safe. And then you can explain to me why you lied to me and were out here in the first place!" she said.

"After everything Mantah Corp. said they'd do to my family, can you blame us for not trusting you?" Sammy said, sitting in Dr. Turner's cave.

"No, I suppose not," Dr. Turner said. "But the work I'm doing is good. How could understanding dinosaurs be bad?"

"Yeah, well, until five minutes ago, you thought those BRADs were just friendly assistants!" Brooklynn pointed out.

"Okay, the BRADs were programmed to protect the biomes," the doctor stated. "I don't think anyone anticipated six kids showing up unannounced!"

Gathering some things, Dr. Turner suddenly said, "Drat. It's almost dinnertime."

"What, you getting takeout?" Kenji joked.

"Dinnertime for the T-rexes," Dr. Turner explained. "I get the rare opportunity to observe mother-daughter eating habits. It's actually . . . surprisingly sweet. Until I can figure out how to ensure your safety, you all remain here."

The doctor left as Darius and Sammy exchanged looks. They waited a minute before leaving the cave, following Dr. Turner.

"Hey, Ben, how about a game?" Yasmina asked.

"Not much of a card person," Ben replied.

"Cool," Yasmina said, the gears in her head turning. "Yeah, cool, uh, then want to help me make some snacks in the kitchen?"

Ben wasn't noticing her sudden interest in him, but Kenji quickly spoke up "I do, Yaz." And then in a whisper, he said, "What is up with you?"

"Just being a good wingman!" Yasmina whispered back. "You totally have a crush on Brooklynn."

"No, I don't! . . . Okay, fine. But even if I do, you're being superweird about it. She's gonna know something's up!"

Yasmina teased him some more.

"Yaz, until I'm ready, can you just . . . chill?" Kenji

begged in a whisper. *"Please?"*

"Odd," Dr. Turner said. "The BRADs usually steer clear when it's feeding time. . . ." She watched as one of the BRADs tended to the feeding platform up ahead.

"So . . . ," came a whisper from behind her. "Do you ring a dinner bell, or—"

Dr. Turner whirled around, stunned to see Darius and Sammy! "What are you— Go back, right now!" she said quietly.

"That's probably more dangerous," Sammy said, "since—"

Dr. Turner hushed Sammy.

"I thought you said the BRADs don't usually come here," Darius said quietly.

"They don't," Dr. Turner replied.

"How many weird things need to happen for you to quit?" Sammy asked as a loud buzz came from the feeding platform, like an alert.

The T. rexes were coming.

"She said they weren't allowed in here!" Ben whispered. He pointed toward the cave entrance as the shadow of a BRAD appeared on the wall!

"Hide!" Kenji said, and the kids scattered. Kenji and Brooklynn ducked behind the kitchen counter, and Yasmina pulled Ben under a worktable.

The BRAD's green scanning light filled the room, narrowly missing the kids.

The robot made its way over to Dr. Turner's desk and sifted through papers. Ben and Yasmina held their breath, hoping the BRAD didn't discover them.

"See, Sammy? How could any of this possibly be a bad thing?" Dr. Turner asked. That's when the doctor noticed something strange. Just as Big Eatie started to eat, Little Eatie shoved her mother out of the way. Then Big Eatie headbutted Little Eatie.

"Odd," Dr. Turner said, looking at the brain scans on her tablet. "Their aggression levels are off the charts. I've never seen this before!"

Little Eatie bit her mother. There was nothing playful about it. Big Eatie chomped at her daughter, leaving a gash on the smaller dinosaur's neck. But Little Eatie didn't seem to care.

"Her pain receptors are dark," Dr. Turner said as she glanced at her tablet. "She can't feel pain! Neither of them can! What is happening?"

"Mantah Corp.," Sammy muttered.

"Hide. I have to call a BRAD to tranquilize them

before they really hurt each other," Dr. Turner said.

Kenji and Brooklynn watched from the kitchen as the BRAD scanned the air right above Yasmina and Ben.

"We have to do something," Brooklynn whispered.

Kenji nodded. He looked behind Brooklynn and noticed a heavy frying pan.

The BRAD examined something on the floor just behind the table where Yasmina and Ben were hiding. All the robot had to do was turn its head and it would discover the kids!

Suddenly, a blanket dropped over the BRAD's head. Kenji swung a frying pan at the robot, and its head flew across the room.

Dr. Turner summoned the BRADs while Darius and Sammy remained hidden, watching the T. rexes charge each another.

Sammy noticed something on top of the food platform as Dr. Turner shouted, "Hide! The BRADs are on the way!"

But there was nowhere *to* hide! Dr. Turner shielded the kids with her body as a BRAD arrived. The robot unleashed a cloud of gas at the T. rexes, and the dinosaurs dropped to the ground and fell fast asleep.

"Do you require anything else, Dr. Turner?" the BRAD asked.

"No," she replied. "Thank you."

The robot left, and Darius and Sammy emerged.

"Let's get out of here," the doctor said.

"Dr. Turner, is this normally in their food?" Sammy said, and she ran over to the food platform. She grabbed something and showed it to Darius and Dr. Turner. It looked like a large cube, about the size of Sammy's hand.

"What happened here?!" Dr. Turner asked as she saw a blanket resting atop a now-headless BRAD.

"It came in a few minutes after you left," Ben explained. "Almost as if it knew you'd be gone."

"It was scanning all over the place," Kenji added.

"It was spying on me," Dr. Turner realized.

"There goes the one place we were supposed to be safe," Sammy said.

"Apologies, Sammy," Dr. Turner said sincerely. "Seems you were right to be suspicious of Mantah Corp."

Looking at the cube Sammy had taken from the feeding platform, the doctor said, "Time to find out what they're doing to my dinosaurs."

In a dark office, someone was staring at a map of the biomes. Red lights were blinking all over it. A light representing one of the BRADs near Dr. Turner's cave stopped blinking, and an error message appeared.

A man sitting in front of a computer screen gasped and shouted, "What? Are you kidding me? Stupid dinosaurs destroyed one of my BRADs?!"

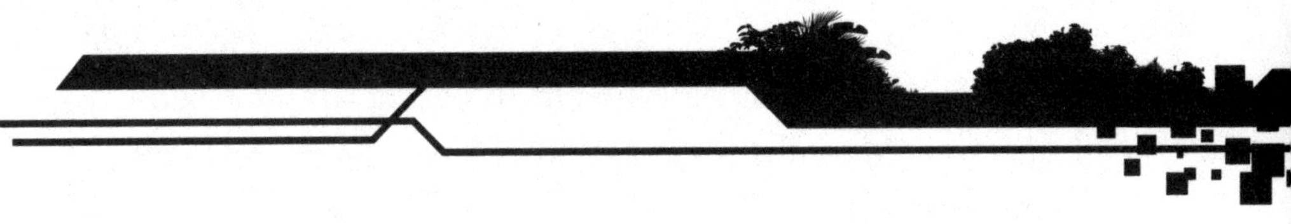

CHAPTER THREE

"This is bad," the doctor said. "Very, very bad."

After further analysis, Dr. Turner announced her findings to the kids. "The T. rexes' food's been tampered with. They're adding things that make the dinos more aggressive and inhibits their ability to feel pain."

"Why would they do that?" Darius wondered.

"No idea," Dr. Turner said. "But it seems it's more important than ever to get you kids off this island."

As the group discussed ways to leave the island, Dr. Turner said, "The supply plane! Only . . . next one's not due for another ten days."

"Any way to make the plane come sooner?" Brooklynn said.

"Well," Dr. Turner replied, thinking. "I suppose it would come if there was some kind of emergency."

"Making emergencies is what we do!" Ben said proudly.

"If we stopped the dinos from eating that messed-up food, Mantah Corp. would notice, right?" Sammy suggested.

"Right," Dr. Turner said, pacing the ground. "All we need is a solid, detailed plan."

"I have an idea," Darius said.

The plan was simple. First, Dr. Turner, Ben, and Kenji waited for the T. rexes to fall asleep. The doctor monitored her tablet for any sign of brain activity.

Second, Brooklynn and Sammy removed all the altered T. rex food from the feeding platform.

Finally, Yasmina and Darius would disable the feeding platform—a move that would hopefully alert Mantah Corp. that something was wrong.

Everything went according to plan.

Except the part about Darius and Yasmina disabling the feeding platform. When the kids got there, they couldn't find any way to wreck it!

"I thought Dr. Turner said there'd be some kind of a power box nearby," Yasmina said.

"It's gotta be here somewhere," Darius said. "Keep looking!"

Meanwhile, hidden in the foliage of a nearby tree, Dr. Turner kept an eye on the dinosaurs' brain patterns.

"They're in a light but restful stage-two sleep," Dr. Turner said. "We just have to be sure—"

Suddenly, Kenji coughed uncontrollably!

The lights on the tablet went wild as Big Eatie stumbled to her feet. Little Eatie tried to stand but was still too weak.

"They should've received medical attention by now," Dr. Turner said, checking her tablet. "Let me put in a request for a med BRAD to—"

Without warning, Big Eatie roared. The dinosaur sniffed, turning toward the food platform.

"Go, go, go!" Ben shouted as they scrambled down the tree. They had to save Darius and Yasmina.

"Found it!" Darius shouted as he pushed back some bushes to reveal a small power box.

Yasmina threw a rock at Darius and said, "Use this!"

Darius caught the rock and smashed it into the power box. A second later, Yasmina joined Darius and started smashing her own rock into the power box. Sparks began to fly, and a moment later, the power box fizzled. So did the feeding platform!

"Time to go!" Kenji hollered as he ran up, the roaring T. rex not far behind.

Darius took off with Ben, but Yasmina stood frozen in fear.

"Yaz, move it!" Kenji urged, grabbing her arm just as Big Eatie arrived. The dinosaur looked at the broken, empty feeding platform and snorted loudly.

"Everyone good?" Darius asked as the group gathered at another spot in the forest.

"It worked!" Dr. Turner said happily. She glanced at her tablet. "The plane will be here in three hours! You lot are almost home."

The kids whooped and hollered.

Just then, a beam of green light sliced through the trees. The light fell right on the kids.

"BRADs," Yasmina said.

A robot emerged from the trees. Its white eye turned red.

Dr. Turner placed herself between the kids and the robot.

"Stop! Wait! Stand down!" she ordered. The robot scanned her.

"Command override due to unauthorized life-forms," the BRAD insisted. "Initiating Elimination Protocol."

"Run!" Dr. Turner yelled. The kids headed into the forest with the BRAD right behind them.

Ben, Darius, Brooklynn, and Sammy led the group,

while Kenji, Yasmina, and Dr. Turner brought up the rear. Yasmina couldn't shake her fear as she ran.

"Keep left!" the doctor yelled. "The airlock to the supply plane's just up ahead!"

Two more BRADs appeared and blocked their path to the airlock.

"How're we gonna get to the plane now?" Yasmina asked.

Dr. Turner took off running. "There's another airlock not far from here. The only challenge is—"

"Look out!" Brooklynn cried. The kids ducked out of the way as a BRAD fired a projectile from its mouth! The orb whizzed by, slamming into a tree trunk. There came a sudden zap of electricity.

"That was waaaaaay too close!" Sammy said as more shock orbs sailed past their heads.

"Split up!" Darius said.

"Just keep eyes on me, everyone!" Dr. Turner added. She kept running for the second airlock as the kids broke off and sprinted in a zigzag, crisscross pattern, still following the doctor.

Confused, the BRADs didn't know where or what to shoot. Every time a robot tried to lock onto one kid, they would pick up another. One of the BRADs crashed into another, knocking it to the ground. Dr. Turner and the kids made it inside the airlock and shut the door behind them.

Then the airlock opened! The three BRADs entered.

"That way to the plane!" Dr. Turner said, pointing up ahead.

"How do we stop the BRADs from following us?" Sammy wondered.

"I have an idea!" Brooklynn said. "You guys go on ahead!"

As the others jumped through the next airlock door, Brooklynn stood in front of the keypad controls.

"Hey!" Brooklynn shouted as one of the BRADs approached. "Unauthorized life-form over here!"

The BRAD locked onto Brooklynn and fired a shock orb right at her! But she drove through the airlock door as it was closing. The shock orb hit the controls, frying the door shut!

Brooklynn rolled to her feet as she listened to the BRADs on the other side, trying—but unable—to get inside!

"Why is it so cold?" Brooklynn wondered as she turned to face her friends. She was shocked to find everyone standing inside an arctic biome!

"I thought you said this was the way to the plane," Yasmina said.

"It is," Dr. Turner insisted. "After we get through this biome. It's cold, but still uninhabited, except for us."

Ben shivered as light snow began to fall.

"None of us will last very long out here," Darius said.

"Yes, we will," Dr. Turner replied as she gestured to two snow glider vehicles off to the side.

The group split up, with Brooklynn, Kenji, and Sammy in one vehicle and Dr. Turner, Yasmina, Ben, and Darius in the other.

Yasmina quickly fell asleep, then woke suddenly.

"Yaz, what is it, hon?" Dr. Turner asked, concerned.

"I . . . ," Yasmina started to say. She wanted to tell the doctor how she was feeling, about the fear growing within her. Instead, she said, "I'm just a little . . . carsick. Weird, huh?"

Dr. Turner could tell there was something else, but now was no time to press the matter.

"Not that weird," Ben said.

"But that is!" Darius shouted, pointing ahead.

Standing there in front of them on the snow-swept landscape, all fifteen feet of her, was a spiked dinosaur!

"Pierce!" the doctor said. "What are you doing out here?!"

Dr. Turner bolted from the snow glider. The shivering creature looked miserable.

"It's a Kentrosaurus," Darius said, climbing out of the vehicle. "They're herbivores."

Pierce fell into the snow, and Dr. Turner checked her pupils. The Kentrosaurus could barely keep her eyes open.

"She's gone into hypothermic shock," she said. "I have to move her out of here."

"What about the supply plane?" Yasmina asked.

"It's coming soon," Dr. Turner said. "You kids take

the gliders and keep going. I'll figure a way to get Pierce back into the desert biome."

"You can't just move a four-thousand-pound dinosaur by yourself," Darius protested.

Brooklynn's eyes met Darius's. "How about some of us go ahead and stall the plane, and the rest can stay back to help?"

Darius considered the plan, then shook his head. "The only way we'll move a dinosaur that big is with both gliders. Right, guys?"

After a moment, the kids agreed—even Yasmina, although she looked less than thrilled.

The group towed Pierce behind the snow gliders. Yasmina checked an alert that popped up on the tablet. "The supply plane's here!"

"I'll pull over," the doctor said. "You take the glider—"

"We're not leaving you, Mae," Darius said. "We can save Pierce and still make the plane if we hurry."

Yasmina couldn't hide her disappointment. Before she could say anything, she saw a BRAD plodding through the snow!

"The airlock's straight ahead," Dr. Turner said as the snow gliders veered away from the BRAD.

The snow gliders headed over a frozen lake. The

weight of the Kentrosaurus caused the ice behind them to crack. The vehicles began to swerve left and right, causing Pierce to swing back and forth. The pursuing BRAD latched on to a glider and charged a shock orb.

Yasmina kicked the BRAD, and it fell into the freezing water! The snow gliders made it safely across the lake, at last reaching the airlock.

Brooklynn and Darius unhitched Pierce from the snow gliders. Dr. Turner opened the airlock door.

"Go," she said. "Get to that plane. *Now.*"

Everyone said their goodbyes and stepped through the airlock, until only Yasmina remained.

"I don't know what's troubling you," Dr. Turner said. "But I do know your friends can help. If you *talk* to them."

Yasmina smiled at the doctor and nodded. Then she raced off through the airlock to rejoin her friends.

Now on a cliff that overlooked the ocean, the kids heard the sound of the seaplane's engines and watched as the plane flew over their heads. They waved and hollered, but it was useless.

The kids had missed the plane.

Darius felt awful. He was the one who had suggested staying to save Pierce.

"This sucks," Yasmina said, slumping against a tree.

As Ben took Darius to check on Dr. Turner, Sammy sat down next to Yasmina.

"Are you okay?" she asked.

"No, Sammy, I'm not," Yasmina said. "I keep having nightmares. I thought it would all be okay if we could just get off Nublar. But here we are, still being hunted. The worst part is, even if we do get home someday, I'm afraid I'll never feel normal again."

Brooklynn looked at her friend and sat down next to her. "You're not alone. I've been having nightmares, too," she said. "Once you've stared down a Dimorphodon, it's hard to forget."

"My nightmares are usually about fire-breathing Compys," Sammy said, then added, *"That can also read your mind!"*

"My worst one is getting stuck with the middle seat on an airplane," Kenji said. "And having to share the armrest with a Scorpios rex."

"I get saving Pierce was the right thing to do," Yasmina said. "But stopping and helping dinosaurs cost us getting home. *Again.* And I'm just tired, and I miss my mom."

Back in the forest biome, a BRAD appeared. Its white eye turned red, and the robot was ready to strike! A man stopped, spun around, and held out a hand with a flat gold ring on one finger.

"It's me," the man said. "Do I *look* like an unauthorized life-form?"

The BRAD beeped. The red eye became white once again. "Negative," the robot replied.

"So how long before that giant walking pincushion bit it in the arctic?"

"Unknown," the robot answered. "The Biorobotic Assistance Droid monitoring the Kentrosaurus went off-line and is nonresponsive."

"Are you telling me we lost a BRAD *and* a dinosaur?" The man screamed.

CHAPTER FOUR

"I'm so sorry," Dr. Turner said. "I don't understand what's going on here, but you have my word that I'll get you off this island somehow."

The others were silent, but Darius spoke. "No. We're not leaving. Obviously, this isn't what we wanted. But we can't quit now. Mantah Corp. doesn't care if they're hurting dinosaurs."

"And, Mae, you can't protect them all on your own," Darius continued. "We have to stay until we fix this."

Yasmina looked behind her, back where they had spotted the plane. "Sure," she said. "Whatever you say. Let's get to work, then. We've gotta get Pierce back to the desert biome. And if the plane's gone, that means the new dinosaur food has already been unloaded."

"We'll go to check the T. rex area to make sure the BRADs haven't tainted their food," Brooklynn said, fist-bumping Kenji.

"Yaz and I are both wrecked, so we're gonna go get

some rest if that's cool," Sammy said.

Brooklynn and Kenji nodded and agreed to meet at Dr. Turner's cave when they were done.

"Nothing," the man said, staring into the hole in the ice. "I gave you guys military-grade processing units, and lizards with the intelligence of a banana are outsmarting you."

The man bent down, staring at patterns on the ice that led away from the hole. "Are those . . . vehicle tracks?" he asked.

The BRAD scanned the ice. "Unknown."

"Okay, then," the man said, frustrated. "Can you at least tell me if the missing BRAD fell through the ice and is down there somewhere?"

The robot scanned the hole. "Due to ice thickness and water depth, location of BRAD is—"

The man kicked the BRAD, then stalked back to the snow glider. "Unknown."

Dr. Turner was doing her best to keep the Kentrosaurus calm. But the animal brayed and flailed. Snatching her tablet, the doctor pressed a colored key on the screen. The trumpet-like sound of a dinosaur call played. Pierce heard the noise. Dr. Turner pressed the key again. "Stop!" she ordered. Pierce looked at Dr. Turner as the dinosaur roared softly. A button on the tablet lit up.

"Scared," the doctor said, reading the tablet. She looked Pierce in the eye as she pressed another key, and a different dinosaur call played. A moment later, Pierce made the same sound. The doctor moved toward Pierce and cuddled her head. "That's right. Home."

Darius was stunned. "She just talked to a dinosaur!"

The sound of machinery filled the air as the feeding platform rose. A BRAD arrived, carrying cubes of food laced with the chemical, and placed them on the platform along with untainted food.

Once the robot left, Brooklynn and Kenji appeared from some nearby bushes and removed the laced cubes from the platform.

Then came the roar as Big Eatie approached the platform. She grabbed a hunk of food and carried it into the forest.

Brooklynn and Kenji followed and saw the T. rex take the food to Little Eatie. The mother roared softly, dropped the food, and nudged it toward her daughter.

"She's still hurt," Kenji said. "I thought Mae sent the BRADs to help her."

"Guess they didn't get the order," Brooklynn replied.

"C'mon, we gotta tell Mae about this." Kenji looked at the dinosaurs sadly as Brooklynn took his hand and squeezed it. Looking into her eyes, he smiled.

"So now is when you decide to just drop 'Oh yeah, I can speak to dinosaurs, but whatevs?' " Darius said. He was walking alongside Ben and Dr. Turner as she led Pierce.

"I guess hiding my personal side project from you all isn't necessary anymore." She chuckled. "I was waiting to develop the research more before I shared it with Mantah Corp. Not sure I'm doing that now."

"Yeah," Ben said. "I'd follow that instinct."

"Yaz, wake up," Sammy whispered. "There's someone here."

Once Sammy and Yasmina had returned to Dr. Turner's cave, they had fallen asleep. A sound startled Sammy awake. She was sure she had heard someone say "Search everything."

Then came the thumping of footsteps, and Sammy scrambled under the bed, yanking Yasmina along with her.

A BRAD entered and began to search the sleeping area. Just as it was about to scan under the bed, a man's nasal voice rang out. "Anything in here?"

"No new documents have been located," the BRAD replied.

"Toss the other rooms, then," the voice said. "Now!"

The robot left the sleeping area. Sammy began to shake. "I know that voice," she said.

Peeking out from the sleeping area, they saw a man sitting in Dr. Turner's chair. The robot brought a notebook to the man. He flipped through the pages, smiling.

Then he got up from the chair and left the cave. The BRAD followed.

"Sammy, what is it?" Yasmina said.

"I have to tell you something," Sammy said.

Pierce struggled across the desert biome. They were getting closer to the food platform, and the dinosaur was even more upset.

"Calm down, Pierce. Calm down," Dr. Turner said. "We're almost to the food platform. Poor thing has to be starving." She pressed a button on the tablet repeatedly. "Safe," she said. "Safe. Safe."

Just then, Brooklynn and Kenji appeared.

"Little Eatie is still hurt," Brooklynn said. "The med BRADs you called never went to help her."

Darius thought for a moment. "How could your orders be overridden?" he said, looking at the doctor.

"I thought there was no communication on or off the island."

Dr. Turner thought for a moment and checked her tablet. "There isn't," she said. "Someone must be here giving counterorders. Kash."

"Who's Kash?" Kenji asked.

"My boss," Dr. Turner replied. "Right, then. You get Pierce to her food. Kash'll be in the jungle biome. I'll get cleaned up, then get some answers."

As the doctor headed off, Ben called out, "You sure that's safe?"

"Until I know what he's up to," Mae said, "best that he doesn't know you all are here."

"Be careful, Mae," Darius said. He turned his attention to the Kentrosaurus. "Come on, Pierce. Let's get some chow."

The doctor paused, then walked back and handed her tablet to Darius. "This is the key for 'safe,' " she said, pointing at the screen. "She may not listen to you, but you can try. I'll be back soon."

"Where's Mae?" Sammy asked as she and Yasmina joined the others.

"She went to see her boss in the jungle biome," Darius answered. "Some guy named—"

"Kash," Sammy said curtly, cutting Darius off.

"How'd you know?" Brooklynn wondered.

Sammy glared at Brooklynn and said, "I'm gonna go confront him and get some answers!"

Kenji raised his hands. "Whoa! Now?" he said, incredulous.

"But Mae said—" Darius protested.

Pierce began to panic, and everyone turned to look at the distressed Kentrosaurus.

Yasmina faced her friend and said, "Sammy, I know how mad you must be, but maybe we should wait—"

But Sammy wasn't having it. "All we *do* is wait! I'm tired of it."

"Mae said we should stay put," Darius stated.

"No!" Sammy cried. "You don't get it! Kash . . . Kash is the one who blackmailed my family!"

The group was silent for a moment, taking in Sammy's shocking revelation.

"I can't imagine how you feel right now," Brooklynn said softly.

"But we won't get the truth by confronting a guy like that," Darius insisted.

Sammy stared at Darius with a wounded look. "How do you all not get this? I thought you were my friends!"

"Sammy, no! You can't!" Darius said.

"You don't get to make decisions about what I do!" Sammy said with fury in her voice.

Pierce became even more agitated. As the group

attempted to calm the dinosaur, Ben said, "Uh, guys? Where's Sammy?"

She was nowhere to be seen.

Dr. Turner stood outside Kash's compound. Two BRADs accompanied her as she approached the entrance. Suddenly, she heard snarling. When she looked up, two Velociraptors appeared! There didn't seem to be any gates or fences around them.

The Raptors jumped, and Dr. Turner backed into Kash as he approached.

"The drones project an invisible fence," Kash said smugly. "Raptors get too close and BZZZZT!"

Kash grinned, then tossed some meat to the Raptors. The dinosaurs snarled but didn't go for the food.

Nervous, Dr. Turner kept her attention on the Raptors. Just as she was about to speak, Kash pulled out her notebook. Her eyes went wide.

"Communicating with dinosaurs? Whoa, Mae," Kash said. "You've been busy."

Sammy had just opened the airlock door to the jungle biome. Taking a deep breath, she looked at the surrounding jungle, and then ran ahead, leaving Darius and the others far behind.

"Why are you spying on me?" Dr. Turner demanded. "And why are you trying to kill my dinosaurs?"

"No need to come in so hot, Mae," Kash said. "Let's just dialogue for a sec."

But Dr. Turner eyed the man with distrust. "You have no intention of making this island a research facility, do you?" she said.

Kash grinned. "Let's just say Mantah Corp. plans here are . . . fluid." Then he tapped on Dr. Turner's notebook. "This research of yours, Mae. Wow. You've opened my eyes to possibilities that I never imagined. And I can imagine a lot."

"Why are you doing this?" Dr. Turner said, shaking her head. "I won't let you use my research for whatever sick plan you've got."

"You won't *let* me?"

"You heard me," the doctor said defiantly. ""I'll go over your head to *you know who.*"

"Is that a threat?" Kash asked ominously.

Sammy sprinted toward Kash's compound, her fists

balled up. She could see Dr. Turner talking to the man.

Before she could take another step, something knocked her down.

"What are you doing?!" Sammy said as Yasmina rolled off her. The other kids pulled Sammy behind a stand of trees.

"Sammy, you'll get answers for your family," Yasmina said. "But you're *our* family, and we're gonna protect you."

"Guys, shhh!" Kenji said, pointing at the drones hovering over Dr. Turner and Kash. "Look!"

Kash faced the BRADs that had accompanied Dr. Turner. With a heavy sigh, he said, "I really wish you didn't make this so . . . adversarial. A couple geniuses like us? We could've made an amazing team."

"Kash," Dr. Turner began. "What are you—"

"Is he . . . ," Kenji whispered.

"No," Brooklynn said softly. "He wouldn't!"

"Okay," Darius said, realizing they needed a plan. "Listen up. . . ."

"Thank you for your contributions to Mantah Corp., Dr. Turner," he said with finality. "But the company has decided to go in a different direction. Your services are—"

But before Kash could finish his sentence, Mae had already taken off!

"Well," Kash said to the BRADs, annoyed. "Go get her."

Without a word, the robots gave chase as Kash smiled to himself. He headed toward his compound, passing the hungry Raptors. Then he stopped, as if an idea had just crossed his mind. Entering the compound, he activated something on a ring he wore.

A few seconds later, the sound of drones could be heard as they glided into view.

Kenji hurled a rock at one of the BRADs as the robot caught sight of him and Brooklynn.

"Unauthorized life-forms. Initiating Elimination Protocol," the robot announced before chasing after the kids. Darius, Sammy, and Yasmina snatched some of the unwatched food.

Kenji and Brooklynn charged the BRAD guarding Dr. Turner! The robot chasing the pair fired a shock orb. The kids dodged the blast, and the same orb took out the other BRAD.

"Mae! Run!" Brooklynn cried out.

The BRAD tried to give chase, but the shock orb was slowing it down.

The second BRAD continued after Kenji and Brooklynn into the jungle.

The drones flying above the Raptors suddenly departed. The dinosaurs took notice and inched forward cautiously. When nothing happened, they took a few more steps. There was no barrier.

They were free.

As they raced through the biome, Dr. Turner appeared momentarily confused—everything was happening so fast! "What are you—" she said.

"We're heading for the airlock!" Sammy answered.

Yasmina sped up as she ran from a BRAD. The robot blasted at her repeatedly, each shot getting closer and closer than the last. She thought that every step might be her last.

Suddenly, a large rock fell from a tree and smashed the BRAD! Stunned, Yasmina watched as Ben dropped down from the branches, smiling at his friend.

Meanwhile, Brooklynn and Kenji took cover as the other BRAD fired at them over and over. The robot was relentless. The thing turned its head slowly, and that's when Brooklynn and Kenji saw Darius standing behind the robot!

With a large branch, Darius took a swing at the BRAD, incapacitating it.

A moment later, Sammy and Dr. Turner arrived at the airlock. The door opened with a WHOOSH, only to reveal another BRAD standing there!

Instinctively, Sammy and Dr. Turner quickly ducked, taking cover.

"I don't think it saw us," Sammy said. Then, after a moment's thought, she whispered, "All right, if we can surprise that thing, we can take it out."

"Noted," Mae whispered back. Grabbing a branch, the doctor headed for the BRAD.

"Wait!" Sammy said. "Mae!"

Before Dr. Turner could strike, the BRAD's eye turned red. Just as it was about to fire, a Raptor leaped on the robot, knocking it down! The dinosaur clamped its jaws onto the BRAD, whipping its head furiously. When it came up, the Raptor held a mass of wires and robot parts in its mouth.

Dr. Turner smacked the Raptor with the branch, shoving the dinosaur back. She took off her jacket and threw it at the Raptor, trying to keep the creature at bay.

Then she swatted at the Raptor once more, but this time, the dinosaur simply clawed the makeshift weapon away and lunged for the doctor.

Dr. Turner raised an arm to defend herself, but she was no match for the Raptor. The dinosaur pierced her arm and torso, taking her down!

The kids grabbed the injured doctor and fled.

The kids carried the unconscious Dr. Turner away from the warring Raptors and robot and found a cave in the jungle. The group was silent for a while, until at last, Brooklynn spoke. "You facing Kash wasn't about it being the brave thing to do," she said, turning to Sammy. "It was about whether it was the smart thing to do."

"Easy, B.," Yasmina said, sticking up for her friend. "If Sammy didn't do what she did, we wouldn't have been there to save Mae."

"It's okay, Yaz," Sammy said softly. "She's right. The only way for us all to get the answers we want is to play the long game."

"Then that's what we'll do," Darius said.

"Hello?" Kash said, speaking into the phone, holding a torn jacket. It looked like the Raptors had whoever had been wearing it. He grinned.

But unnoticed by Kash, hidden in some nearby bushes, was Ben, who had witnessed the whole episode. "Kash has a phone," he whispered, amazed.

CHAPTER FIVE

Sammy knelt over the injured doctor. "We gotta do something."

"Kash has a phone!" Yasmina replied. "We get it, call for help, and get out of here!"

"Yaz is right," Brooklynn said. "We gotta find Kash and wait for our chance to grab that phone."

"Let's split up and try to find Kash," Ben said.

A whir cut through the silence, and everyone grew quiet. When they looked out of the cave, they saw two BRADs. Suddenly, the robots said, "New orders received."

The robots retreated, each heading in a different direction.

"One of them could be headed to Kash," Yasmina noted.

"Only one way to find out," Brooklynn said.

Ben looked at his friends. "You guys go. I think

there was a first aid kit in the snow gliders. I'll get Mae patched up."

The kids nodded. Brooklynn and Yasmina followed one BRAD, and Darius, Sammy, and Kenji took the other.

Yasmina and Brooklynn kept enough distance that the robot wouldn't detect them. They watched as the robot entered a warehouse. A moment later, they slipped inside as well. The door closed behind them, and the kids found themselves in near darkness. It took a couple of minutes for their eyes to adjust, and the first thing Yasmina saw was a BRAD right in front of her!

"They're inactive," Brooklynn whispered, pulling Yasmina behind a crate.

The BRAD they had followed now crossed to the other side of the warehouse, passing a man hunched over an inactive robot. The BRAD stopped and powered down.

"Kash?" Yasmina mouthed.

Brooklynn nodded and motioned to move in for a closer look.

In the forest biome, Darius, Kenji, and Sammy saw the robot they were following enter a clearing where Big Eatie was nursing Little Eatie back to health. The robot scanned the smaller dinosaur.

"Health readings suboptimal," the BRAD stated. "Unsuitable for test."

It then scanned the larger T. rex. "Subject suitable for test."

"What test?" Darius whispered.

Without warning, Big Eatie grabbed the BRAD in her jaws and shook the robot, smashing it to pieces!

Yasmina and Brooklynn hid behind a crate right next to Kash's workstation. They noticed a computer on a table as Kash screwed a panel into place on the inactive BRAD. When he finished, the robot's eye lit up.

"Prepare the test space outside my compound," Kash commanded.

The robot's eye flashed blue. "Unable to connect to drone perimeter system," it answered.

"Retry connection protocol," Kash sighed.

"Unable to connect to drone perimeter system," the BRAD repeated.

"Gah!" Kash said, exasperated. "Fine! Like everything else, I'll do it myself."

Throwing the screwdriver to the floor, Kash moved to the computer. He took off his jacket, setting it on the crate in front of Brooklynn. She saw the phone in his pocket!

Brooklynn reached out for the phone as Kash banged on the keyboard. She flinched, yanking her hand back.

"No connection, either?!" Kash shouted, hurling the computer monitor against the wall.

Brooklynn nearly had the phone when Kash suddenly snatched his jacket away.

Kash then left the warehouse. The BRAD followed him.

Yasmina looked like she was about to faint. She was so scared, and Brooklynn had almost gotten caught!

"It's okay," Brooklynn said. "We can go back if you want."

"No," Yasmina said, taking a deep breath. "We should follow him."

Brooklynn nodded, and they left the warehouse.

Four drones appeared above, encircling Big Eatie—then they zapped her. The dinosaur roared in pain. She snarled as she was driven away from her offspring. The big dinosaur staggered away from the spot where

Darius, Kenji, and Sammy had been hiding.

The kids followed closely as the drones continued to herd the dinosaur away. Soon, the drones were joined by multiple BRADs.

Darius wanted to help the T. rex. But there was no way they could take on the drones alone.

"Darius, let's go," Sammy said. "Kash and his phone aren't here. Maybe Brooklynn and Yaz had more luck. C'mon!"

Darius's heart sank at the sight of Big Eatie in pain. Reluctantly, he followed his friends.

Brooklynn and Yasmina returned to the cave empty-handed. They had followed Kash to his compound but were forced to turn back by the Raptors. In the cave, they found Ben and a freshly bandaged Dr. Turner. While they were gone, Ben had made his way to the arctic biome and retrieved the first aid kit and some bottled water from the snow gliders. He cleaned Dr. Turner's wounds and bandaged them as best he could.

"We found Kash," Yasmina said. "In this creepy warehouse full of BRADs."

"I almost had the phone," Brooklynn said. "But then—"

At that moment, Darius, Kenji, and Sammy returned.

"The BRADs forced Big Eatie away from her daughter," Darius said, clearly upset. "She's hurt pretty bad. Big Eatie fought to stay, but they shocked her until she left with them. . . . He wants to use her for some kind of test."

The cave grew silent, and a familiar braying could be heard outside. The buzzing of drones followed.

"That's Pierce!" the doctor said. She tried to get up, but the kids stopped her.

"We'll go," Darius said. "You need to rest."

"But if Kash is hurting her—"

"Don't worry. I won't let him," Darius said. He exchanged a concerned look with Dr. Turner as he left the cave with the others.

"Let's see what we're working with," Kash said, accessing the computer.

"Good afternoon, Kash," an automated voice replied as a screen lit up. Kash raised an arm, and music began to play. Then he lifted his other arm, and an app opened on the large computer screen.

With both arms raised, Kash grinned wickedly.

"What are they doing to her?" Yasmina whispered.

The kids stood outside Kash's compound, peering

through some bushes at Pierce. The dinosaur stamped the ground, braying, as drones hovered above, goading her.

They heard the buzzing of more drones, and the ground began to shake. Big Eatie had arrived.

The drones kept the two dinosaurs on opposite sides of a clearing. Darius thought it resembled a giant boxing ring.

"This is his test," Darius said, feeling sick to his stomach. "He's gonna force them to fight."

"No way," Ben said, disgusted.

"It adds up. Dosing the food, making them more aggressive, seeing how strong they are, Mae's research . . . He doesn't care how dinosaurs feel. He only wanted to know how they'd do in a fight."

Brooklynn looked horrified. "But Pierce is no match for Big Eatie!" she said, and Kenji quietly put his arm around her.

"Guys," Darius began. "I know that phone is our only way to get us and Mae off this island, but we have to—"

"Save those dinosaurs!" Brooklynn said, cutting him off sharply.

The rest of the group chimed in, their agreement unanimous.

Then Yasmina spoke. "This is what's most important."

The buzzing of the drones drew Brooklynn's attention. "Kash must be controlling those drones from his compound. If we can get in there, we can disable them and keep the dinos from hurting each other."

"We'll have to lure Kash out," Darius replied.

"I got some ideas on that front," Ben said.

"Perfect. Sammy, you and I are with Ben. Once Kash leaves his compound—"

Brooklynn threw her arms around Kenji as she said, "We'll trail him. Make sure he stays out."

"Okay," Darius continued. "Yaz, use your speed to get past the Raptors, sneak into the compound, and get control of the drones."

Yasmina gave a sharp nod.

"Are you sure?" Brooklynn said, looking at her friend.

"I got this," Yasmina answered. She took a step forward and felt herself breathing faster, harder. Turning around, Yasmina suddenly couldn't see Darius, or anyone else, for that matter. Her vision had narrowed. She couldn't hear anything except her breathing. What was happening?

Sammy looked over her shoulder and saw Yasmina sitting on the ground, doubled over, her hands on her knees.

"Yaz?" she called out.

Darius watched as Yasmina collapsed.

"Yaz!" Darius screamed as they ran to their woozy friend's side.

"I'm sorry, I just . . . I'm fine."

Now alert, Yasmina rested on the ground. Darius and Sammy were next to her.

At last, she decided to tell the truth.

"I've been having these . . . nightmares," Yasmina said, her voice soft. "That I'm alone, being hunted. When I told the others and found out they've been having them, too, I felt better. But I'm obviously . . . not as fine as I thought."

"Everyone's having nightmares?" Darius said, shocked. "Why didn't anyone tell me?"

"It's not like that, Darius," Sammy replied. "We only just started talking about it after we stopped to save Pierce and . . . missed . . . the plane . . . home."

Darius hung his head.

"And we didn't want you to feel bad, because we *all* agreed it was the right thing to do," Yasmina said. "Just like we're doing now. Of course I want to go home. We all do. But sometimes there are more important things than what we want. Right?"

Darius smiled at his friend, but there was sadness in his eyes.

"New plan," Darius said. "You go with Sammy and Ben. I've got the compound."

Yasmina grinned back at him. "Thanks, D."

Darius took off for the compound. He was trying not to think about what was coming next. A sad but determined grimace replaced the smile he had given his friends.

"Okay," Kash said, checking the heads-up display. "All systems are go. Let's get this party started."

As he waved his arms, the drones outside the compound obeyed.

The silence of the jungle biome was broken by the snow glider. Ben and Yasmina hopped out of the vehicle and hurriedly attached multiple canisters of compressed air to the front of the snow glider. Then they got back in.

"The warehouse is through those trees," Yasmina said. "I guess it's not a Ben plan if it doesn't involve blowing something up."

Sammy slammed on the gas, and the snow glider shot forward.

Then a BRAD stepped right into their path!

Yasmina and Ben recoiled as Sammy drove the snow glider into the robot, flipping it over the top of their vehicle. With a loud crash, the BRAD landed behind them in a heap.

Sammy and Yasmina high-fived.

Kash grinned with evil intent and watched the dinosaurs start to fight. It was precisely what he wanted.

Suddenly, a red light on the screen went out. It indicated that a BRAD had just been destroyed.

"What?!" Kash growled.

The snow glider skidded to a stop near the warehouse. There were no BRADs to be seen.

"It's now or never," Ben said.

Sammy revved the snow glider's engine and floored it toward the warehouse. At the last possible second, the three dove out of the snow glider, rolling along the jungle floor. The snow glider hit the side of the warehouse, unleashing the compressed air. The explosion shook the trees as thick smoke began to rise.

An impatient Kash glared at the computer screen as every red light in the warehouse winked out. He glanced out the window and saw black smoke rising beyond the tree line.

“What’s with all the interruptions?!” Kash yelled. He dashed out of the compound with a BRAD in tow.

Darius watched them depart. He was just outside the perimeter, near the Raptors, waiting until Kash was gone. The only way to Kash’s office would be through the Raptors’ territory. So Darius ran.

Drawn to his movement, a Raptor raced toward him, its jaws snapping.

Darius made it to the front door. But there was no door*knob!*

He searched for a way to get inside as the Raptor came closer. Finally, he saw a button and pressed it. The door swung open, and Darius jumped in. The Raptor gnashed its teeth, trying to grab Darius as the door closed!

Inside, Darius headed down a hallway until he came to a pair of closed elevator doors at the end. There were UP and DOWN buttons on the control panel. He thought for a moment, then pressed UP. Getting out, he saw an empty hallway. He spied a door at the end and crept toward it quietly.

“What is going on around here?!” Kash shouted as the BRAD kept pace with him.

He stopped, as if remembering something. Kash looked at his watch, then patted his pockets a few times, searching. Whatever he was looking for wasn't there.

"Perfect," he said, frustrated. "And I'm gonna miss my check-in with the big guy."

Kash turned to the BRAD and screamed, "Go back and get my phone!"

The BRAD obeyed, retreating to the compound as Kash headed to the warehouse.

This didn't go unnoticed by Brooklynn and Kenji, who were hiding nearby.

"Oh no," Brooklynn said. "Darius!"

"No way we get past them," Kenji said.

"What about Darius and Yaz?" Brooklynn asked.

"If anyone can think of something," he replied, "it's them."

Darius entered the office full of high-tech computer gear. He looked at the computer screen that showed the drones in the air, keeping their positions.

A loud roar from outside distracted him, and Darius went to the window. Pierce and Big Eatie swung their tails at each other, chomping madly. They looked tired. Pierce stumbled.

"No!" Darius shouted, yearning to stop the fight. He turned his attention back to the computer. As he moved, he saw several items on the screen light up. Raising an eyebrow, Darius stopped moving. Then he slowly raised an arm. The lights moved! So that was how Kash controlled his computer!

Outside in the clearing, Big Eatie snapped her massive jaws at Pierce. Suddenly, the drones—now controlled by Darius—flew in between the two, distracting both creatures.

Sweat trickled down Darius's face as controlled the drones. He heard the sound of the elevator doors opening. Darius ducked behind a couch and nearly gasped when a BRAD entered. The robot went to the fireplace and picked something up.

It was Kash's phone!

Darius stared out the window as he watched the weary Big Eatie and Pierce. The last drones hovered above, just waiting to be moved in order to save the dinosaurs. He looked back at the BRAD holding the phone.

Darius had a choice: save the dinosaurs, or save their chance to finally go home.

"I'm sorry," Darius said softly.

Charging ahead, Darius jumped on the robot! Holding on tight, he tore the phone from the BRAD. The robot stumbled backward, and Darius hit the wall. The phone flew out of his hand!

The BRAD fired a shock orb at him before he could

grab the phone. Darius dove out of the way, then grabbed a golf club from the pile of stuff that Kash had brought with him to the island. He smacked the BRAD in the head with the golf club. The robot staggered, tripped over a rug, and fell to the floor as it shorted out.

Dazed, Darius picked up the phone and dialed a number.

The phone rang.

A loud roar from outside turned his attention back to the window. He saw Pierce, whipping her tail at Big Eatie. He was already heading for the drone controls to try and help when he heard a voice on the other end of the phone say, "Hello?"

"Hello?!" Darius said, his eyes aglow.

Suddenly, the phone was snatched from his hand.

"You are in a lot of trouble," Kash said.

Darius's brother, Brand, sat on the edge of his brother's bed, the phone pressed against his ear.

"Hello?! Darius?" Brand said. "Is that you?!"

He couldn't believe it! He hadn't heard from his brother in months. And now the phone had gone dead. There was no voice on the other end. Brand had tears in his eyes as a smile slowly spread across his face.

"He's alive."

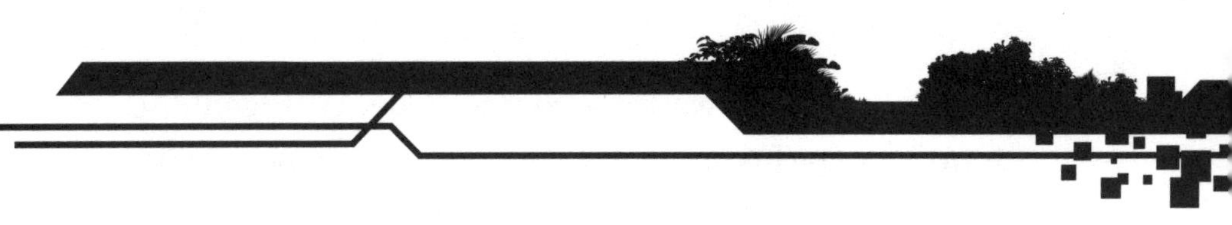

CHAPTER SIX

"Who are you?!" Kash said.

"I'm the luckiest guy alive!" Darius said, thinking fast. "Another human! Finally! I'm saved!"

Darius hugged Kash. Caught off guard, Kash backed away.

"Okay, okay, easy. Just back it up, kid, and answer my questions," Kash said. "Who are you, and *how* did you get on *my island*?"

"My name is Darius Bowman. My boat was destroyed, and I washed up here. I came from Isla Nublar."

"Nice try," Kash said, looking suspicious. "Jurassic World tanked six months ago."

Darius took a deep breath and started to tell a story. "My dad and I were on vacation when that Indominus thing escaped. We hid in these caves for a while, so we missed the evacuation. After that, we had to fight for our lives every day."

What he said wasn't a complete lie. With genuine emotion, Darius said, "My dad . . . didn't make it. I've been on my own ever since."

"You expect me to believe that?" Kash snorted.

"It's the truth!" Darius insisted. "Look, man, if you let me call someone, anyone, I'm more than happy to get outta your way and go the heck home."

Kash gave Darius a sinister look.

"What can we do?" Sammy said helplessly, watching the dinosaurs battle. "Big Eatie and Pierce are gonna kill each other!"

Pierce tried to get away, but the drones prevented her exit. The only way to give the dinosaurs a chance was to knock those drones out of the sky.

Sammy and Yasmina went one way, while Brooklynn and Kenji went another.

Brooklynn and Kenji scrambled up a tree and inched out, getting closer to a hovering drone. Brooklynn took a stick in one hand and swung at the drone! The device must have been sensitive to the motion, because it zoomed out of the way.

Glancing at a branch above them, Brooklynn said, "Can you go up any higher?"

Kenji sighed. "Fine," he said, and he started climbing.

The campers finally get off the island, narrowly escaping Dr. Wu . . .

. . . and his goons.

Life on the boat is neither easy . . .

. . . nor tasty. YUCK!

A storm drives Darius and his friends ashore to . . .

. . . another island!

The new island is less hospitable than the last.

It seems deserted until they find . . .

. . . a robotic arm?!

A sandstorm sends them deeper into the island.

They set up camp in the hopes of getting some rest.

But there's something in the darkness . . .

. . . a saber-toothed tiger!

Darius and his friends make more discoveries . . .

. . . mainly that the island is definitely *not* uninhabited!

"You're telling me you destroyed an entire warehouse of BRADs on your own?" Kash said.

"The robots who kept trying to kill me? You bet I did," Darius answered.

"Uh-huh," Kash said, still not buying it. "And how did you get past my Raptors?"

"The ones outside? *Pffft,*" Darius said, acting cool. "I've dealt with way worse than that. How do you think I survived so long on Nublar?"

Kash stood there, quiet, considering Darius's story. He was interrupted by a pained roar from outside. Turning toward the window, Kash watched Pierce and Big Eatie fight.

"Whoa," Darius said. Despite being sickened by watching the dinosaurs fight, he pretended to be amazed.

"Cool, right?" Kash said, picking up on Darius's enthusiasm.

"Supercool. Dinosaurs took *everything* from me," Darius lied. "I'm all about watching them go at each other for a change."

That, Kash seemed to believe.

"It'll be over soon, though," Kash said. He stared at a screen, checking the dinosaurs' aggression and exhaustion levels. "The T. rex is still amped up, and the Kentro's whipped."

Darius felt awful. He looked at the phone in Kash's pocket, then out the window.

Kenji had made it to the higher branch and was now above Brooklynn. She took another swing at the drone. It moved to avoid Brooklynn's blow and ended up right in Kenji's reach! He knocked the drone from the sky.

Suddenly, one of the drone dots on Kash's monitor turned red. He looked out the office window, but he couldn't see the drone.

"Ugh," Kash moaned. "Drone must've flown too close to the tree. Sensors need an upgrade."

Kash kept his attention focused on the monitor, while Darius squinted out the window. He was sure that he saw a rock flying past another drone!

On the ground, Ben and Yasmina were hidden by trees. Using bandages from the first aid kid like slingshots, they fired rocks at the drones.

Sammy threw rocks to them, keeping the pair supplied with ammunition. Ben grazed a drone, but it only made the device wobble.

Darius noticed the wobbly drone. He realized that his friends were trying to free the dinosaurs! Kash then turned toward the window, and Darius knew he had to distract him.

"So what's the deal?" Darius asked. "You just fight 'em . . . to the death?"

"Problem with that?" Kash said.

"Nah, just wondering. You must have a ton of dinosaurs here."

Kash gave him a side glance. "Whaddya mean?" he said suspiciously.

"I figure making them is crazy expensive, but if you lose one every fight, you either have a lot of 'em or a ton of dough."

"Actually," Kash said with a sigh," they are pretty expensive."

At least Darius now knew that Kash wasn't the only one behind whatever was going on here.

With a well-placed shot, Sammy, Ben, and Yasmina

finally managed to take down another drone.

But Big Eatie and Pierce were still fighting.

There was now a gap in the drones, but the dinosaurs didn't realize they could flee through that space.

Suddenly, Big Eatie rammed into Pierce, knocking the dinosaur onto her side. Pierce attempted to get up, roaring in pain, then dropped back down.

The kids felt something heavy thudding their way, and they hid as BRADs stormed toward the dinosaurs. Big Eatie roared, ready to strike at the fallen Pierce.

But before the T. rex could act, the BRADs sprayed gas, rendering the dinosaurs unconscious almost immediately.

"Wonder why he stopped them," Ben said.

Kash took his finger off the SLEEPING GAS button on his computer screen. "I guess the boss will be happier if they can fight again," he said. "Might already be too late for the Kentrosaurus."

Darius smiled at him, but inside, he felt terrible.

"I'm Kash, by the way," the man said. "Now, what am I gonna do with you?"

A few minutes later, Kash led Darius out of the compound and across the clearing. Two BRADs flanked them on either side. They were heading toward the site of the T. rex–Kentrosaurus battle.

"He's out!" Brooklynn gasped, pointing at Darius.

"But Kash has him," Yasmina said.

Darius had no idea that at that moment, his friends were watching him from a distance. "Where are we going?" he asked.

"Look, kid," Kash said. "I got stuff to do, and I'm not letting you out of my sight. So don't be annoying and don't even *think* of trying to escape. The minute it's easier to just feed you to a dinosaur, that's exactly what I'll do."

The other kids followed Darius and Kash, making sure they weren't seen.

Moments later, Darius and Kash were at the spot where the dinosaurs had been fighting. Pierce was already gone, and BRADs were loading Big Eatie onto a platform.

Kash gave Darius a nudge, ordering him to step onto the platform with the T. rex.

The kids watched as the platform lowered into the ground and Darius, Kash, and the T. rex fell from their view.

"Mae might know where they went," Brooklynn said.

Darius gasped when the platform reached its destination. He was now inside an enormous, state-of-the-art dinosaur care facility! The place was large enough to accommodate dinosaurs of all different shapes and sizes. A calming blue light illuminated the space. Darius noticed huge, dinosaur-sized doors throughout. There was also a computer center, what looked like an operating room, and cabinets for supplies.

"Whoa," Darius said. "I was wondering where those platforms went. You got a genetics lab down here, too?"

"So many questions," Kash said. "*Too* many questions."

"Hey, man," Darius replied. "I'm just looking out for me. If I'm stuck here, I just want to know you got this handled better than those fools on Nublar."

Kash took that as a challenge. "Once this place is up and running, it'll make Jurassic World look like a cheap knockoff. Dinosaurs are only here to fight for the entertainment of serious high rollers."

Darius nodded. "Nice. What's with the different terrains and junk?"

"Why watch dinos only fight in the jungle, when you can also watch 'em duke it out in the snow or the desert or somewhere else?" Kash explained. "If you can afford it, we can provide it."

"That is so dope," Darius said as he fist-bumped Kash.

Darius noticed that Kash smiled. He hoped that he could keep up his act.

"There's an underground med bay," Dr. Turner said, sitting up in the cave. "I didn't have access, probably because Kash is doing horrible things he didn't want me to know about."

"We need another way to get in," Brooklynn said.

"Any of the feeding platforms should get you down to the lower level," Dr. Turner replied as she checked her tablet. "The next feeding is in the desert."

"What should we do?" Sammy said as the kids all looked to Brooklynn for an answer.

"We go get Darius," Brooklynn said. "No matter what."

Kash focused on a computer console while a BRAD stood next to him. Darius wondered how he could sneak away.

"So all these doors are, like, rooms for injured dinosaurs?" he asked innocently.

"No, they're mega-garages for ginormous cars," Kash replied sarcastically. "Yes, they're rooms. Stop talking!"

Kash returned to the computer and typed away.

Darius inched away from his captor. But he stopped in his tracks when he caught sight of Big Eatie, still asleep.

"I'm sorry," he whispered to the T. rex. "I could've stopped it, but I just wanted to get my friends home. If I had chosen differently—"

"Hey!" Kash shouted.

Darius flinched, thinking he was caught. But Kash wasn't talking to him—he was on the phone.

"Boss man!" Kash said. "I know, yes, of course, you're not a fan of the nickname. But—yes, the dino fights are coming along. However, sir, I have an even bigger idea I wanna run by you. . . ."

Kash walked away to continue his call, and the BRAD followed him.

Darius looked at Big Eatie and saw that one of Pierce's spikes was embedded in her hide. He reached for the spike and started to pull.

Suddenly, the T. rex's eyes opened, and she stared right at Darius! He held his breath, then slowly removed the spike. He said softly, "I'm just trying to help. Okay?"

Once the spike was out, Big Eatie seemed to relax. A little more confident, Darius touched Big Eatie, trying to comfort the T. rex.

Darius snuck around Big Eatie as he watched Kash pace near the computer.

"Dino battles will make bank for sure, but if you'll

listen, my idea could propel Mantah Corp. into the next stratosphere!" Kash said, pulling the phone away from his ear as the person on the other end yelled. "Yeah, okay—I hear ya loud and clear. 'Stick to your plan and stop wasting time.' "

Darius was heading for a door when Kash hung up the phone and went back to the computer.

"We're doing another test," Kash sighed. "Put Asset 87 in the desert. Monitor its stats. See how long it can last in the heat or whatever."

"I am not sure how to quantify 'whatever,' " the BRAD replied, tilting its head.

"Just. Do. The test," Kash said, annoyed.

Darius was nearly out the door when the BRAD came toward him! Ducking out of the way, he watched as the door opened and the robot left. Glancing at Kash, Darius made a break for it.

But it closed before he could leave! Then he heard the sound of something small and metallic banging off a wall right next to his head—it was a soda can! Darius panicked.

It took him a second to realize that Kash hadn't thrown the can at him. Kash was just angry. He slammed his chair to the floor as he screamed, "Why. Is *he*. In charge?!"

"If you ask me, dude sounds like a total jerk," Darius said, distracting Kash.

"I didn't," Kash said snidely. Then a moment later

he added, "But he is."

"I don't know what your idea is," Darius said. "But he should listen to you. Sure, dino fights are cool . . . for a while. After that, it's gonna get lame."

Kash walked over to Darius, then grinned, slapping him on the back.

"Exactly," Kash said.

"What are you looking for?" Darius asked. He watched as Kash searched through the med bay like a wild man.

"Holler if you see a case labeled 'V55 CHIPS,' " he said, looking through some cabinets. "Never mind. Found it."

Kash gave the case to the BRAD. But the robot dropped the box, and it hit the floor, chips spilling everywhere. Darius helped Kash pick up the chips. Unnoticed, he managed to slide one into his pocket. With the chips returned to the box, Kash threw it into another box, along with various items he had gathered from his desk.

"Anything else I can do to help?" Darius asked.

"Unless you can reprogram a multicore processor in less than a week, then no," Kash said, scoffing.

"Why do you need to do that?" Darius pressed.

"Some science type who used to work here came up with a sorta dinosaur language," Kash said as he continued to gather items. "I figured, if they can understand what I'm saying, what's to stop me from making them *do* whatever I want?"

Then he gave Darius a particularly cruel grin. "I'm talking completely controlling dinosaurs," Kash continued. "Imagine the kind of power you'd have if these stone-cold killers did your bidding? No one is saying no to you ever again."

Darius was practically in shock as he said, *"Siiiick."*

While Darius was busy with Kash, the other kids entered the desert biome and made their way to a feeding platform. Entering the hole, they found a network of underground tunnels beneath the biomes.

Racing down a tunnel, they looked at Dr. Turner's tablet.

"The med bay should be straight ahead!" Brooklynn said. She only hoped they would be in time to save Darius.

Carrying the box of supplies, Kash led Darius over to an elevator.

"I'm gonna be busy for the next few days, so if you stay outta the way and don't distract me, you just might survive this," Kash said. "Sound good?"

He entered the elevator after Kash, and the doors closed.

At that moment, the kids burst into the med bay—on the other side of the room! Kash couldn't see them over the box, but Darius did. As the doors closed, Darius jumped out of the elevator.

"Where are you going?!" Kash shouted. But the doors had already closed.

An angry Kash hammered on the DOWN button. But the elevator was still going up!

"Kash is planning on using Mae's language to control the dinosaurs," Darius said, filling his friends in on the situation.

"How?!" Kenji wondered.

"Don't know," Darius replied. "But the only way to find out or try to stop it is if . . ."

Brooklynn finished Darius's thought. "You stay here."

They didn't want to leave Darius with a dangerous person like Kash, but they also knew it was the only way.

"If I run now, he'll hunt me down and find the rest of you," Darius said. "But if I'm on the inside . . ."

"You can find a way to get us information," Brooklynn said. “Then we can do whatever we can to undo Kash’s plans.”

Sammy glanced over at the elevator and noticed that the car was returning. “Guys, he’s coming back!” she said.

A moment later, the elevator doors were opening. Kash kicked them impatiently.

“You’re toast, little man!” Kash fumed. “I’m gonna—”

Kash stopped talking as he saw Darius standing there. Darius held a V55 chip—the one he had pocketed earlier.

“Saw this on the floor,” Darius said, smiling innocently. “Thought you might need it.”

Brandon Bowman couldn’t move fast enough as he hurriedly threw clothes into a bag. Then he looked at his brother’s room. He was determined to find Darius and bring him back home.

CHAPTER SEVEN

Several days later, Kash sat in front of a computer, looking at the chip in his right hand. "Out with the old . . . in with the cool."

As he kissed the new chip, the phone rang. Darius had already snuck out of the office and was heading down the hall when he heard the phone. For the last week, he had been meeting up with his friends every other night to update them on anything he found out. So far, it wasn't much.

Slipping back toward the computer room, Darius listened in on Kash's conversation.

"The investors are coming? *Nice!* Listen, Boss. The Kash-meister is gonna blow their minds. They'll beg us to take their money."

There was a pause, and then Kash said, "Six days? That is not a lot of time to get the biomes and dinos prepared. Yeah—no—I got this. The future of the company could *not* be in better hands."

Darius grinned—at last, he had some info to share! He heard Kash hang up and a noise that sounded like somebody punching a wall.

He kept walking, heading for the elevator.

"There he is!" Kenji said. But just as Darius emerged from the compound, a sleek, black BRAD appeared. Except this model was much larger and walked upright, almost like a T. rex. The new robot fired an explosive orb! The blast threw Darius to the ground.

Kenji wanted to run and help his friend, but Brooklynn held him back.

Kash arrived a moment later, a golf club slung over his shoulder. "I see you've found your new babysitter," he said. "Or rather, it's found *you*. It's part of my new fleet of upgraded models. I call it BRAD-X."

Darius pushed himself up off the ground.

"After you disappeared, it seemed like a good time to take this baby for a spin," Kash continued. "BTdubs, what *are* you doing out here?"

"Honestly?" Darius said, nervous. He hoped that Kash hadn't figured out what he was really up to. "I've been cooped up all day. Can't I go for a walk?"

"Sure you can," Kash said. "And BRAD-X will be right

there with you. And in case you get any ideas . . ."

Kash bashed the robot repeatedly with his golf club. When he finished, there wasn't even so much as a dent in the robot's armored hide.

"This new model's virtually indestructible."

Darius glanced over his shoulder at his friends. He quickly flashed six fingers to his friends.

"What does that mean?" Kenji wondered.

"No idea," Brooklynn said. "But we need to know what Darius knows."

Darius watched as Kash worked feverishly at the computer, inputting line after line of code.

"Anything I can help with?" he asked.

"Know what?" Kash said, like an idea had just come to him. "Maybe you can be useful."

"Yeah!" Darius said. "What do you need?"

"First thing in the a.m., go clean up the jungle biome. Normally, I'd have the BRADs do it, but thanks to you, I'm a little shorthanded," Kash said. "*If* you can handle that, I've got something *much bigger* for you."

"No problem!" Darius said with a big smile, hoping he'd meet up with his friends. "I'm on it!"

As he started to leave the office, Kash added, "And if you try anything funky . . . well, BRAD-X will show you why that's a *painfully* bad idea."

“That coward turned a robot loose on a child?!” Dr. Turner said as Ben checked on her wounds.

“Kash went to town on it, and it didn’t even get a scratch!” Kenji observed.

“Just because it’s tough on the outside, doesn’t mean it’s tough on the *inside,* too,” Sammy noted. “It’s just a robot, right? Maybe you can shut it down or reprogram it to be good instead of evil.”

“Could work,” Brooklynn mused. “Kash did say he has a ‘fleet’ of BRAD-Xs.”

“So if we can find one,” Yasmina said, following Brooklynn’s lead, “you can hack it.”

It took a second for Brooklynn to realize that she’d suddenly been volunteered for the job.

“Oh,” she said haltingly. “Uh, not sure if—”

“We’d finally have a way to communicate with Darius!” Ben exclaimed.

“Wow, Brooklynn,” Dr. Turner said. “Is there anything you can’t do?”

Everyone had such confidence in her, but Brooklynn wasn’t so sure. They acted like it was no big deal to reprogram the robot. She hoped she could do it.

Another BRAD-X cruised down a path in the forest biome. Something ahead seemed to draw its attention.

From her hiding spot, Brooklynn signaled Sammy and Kenji to get ready.

Picking them up in its claws, the BRAD-X examined what it had found. They appeared to be broken BRAD parts. A second later, Ben and Yasmina dropped a small log from the tree up above, smacking the robot!

The BRAD-X didn't move, and Brooklynn looked on happily. "Guys! I think it wor—"

But before she could get the words out, the robot stood up!

The kids barely had time to hide as the robot moved along, heading away from the kids.

"Okay," Brooklynn said. "Let's see where it's going."

The kids soon arrived at a different warehouse. They snuck inside, with Brooklynn leading the way. Hiding behind some crates and equipment, they watched as the BRAD-X carried the broken robot parts.

Ben pointed at a row of inert BRAD-Xs. There was a repair BRAD nearby that appeared to be making even more robots. Ben pointed at the repair-bot and whispered, "Brooklynn can't do anything until we take that one out."

The kids ducked down as the BRAD-X they had encountered in the forest passed by and left the workshop. But when they came up, they were shocked to see the repair BRAD staring right at them! No one made a move as the robot's claw reached out toward Brooklynn's face . . . and took a part sitting on top of a crate right next to her. The BRAD didn't even notice her! The robot turned around and went back to building more robots.

"Looks like that BRAD isn't all 'killery' like the rest of them," Sammy surmised.

The kids quickly formulated a new plan. Yasmina and Kenji would keep watch outside the warehouse, to make sure no other BRADs, or Kash, were coming. Ben was going to check on Darius while Brooklynn worked.

Brooklynn picked up some tools and struggled to pry a panel off an inactive BRAD-X, with Sammy assisting.

"I wouldn't even know where to begin," Sammy said, watching her friend. "Good thing you do!"

"I've actually never done anything like this before," Brooklynn said. She had done so many different things that she had documented in her videos—but hacking a robot wasn't one of them.

At last, the panel came off. But the BRAD-X came online, leaning away from them! It crashed to the ground, and the girls were sure the noise would bring trouble. But the repair BRAD just kept on working.

Brooklynn wondered if she could pull this off.

Ben climbed a tree just outside of Kash's compound. He saw the man standing on a rooftop patio with Darius. They both held clubs, driving golf balls into the woods.

WHACK!

A ball sailed past Ben's face.

"Man, I *hate* that guy," Ben muttered as he nestled into his hiding spot to listen.

"*You* are going to inject my new control chip into a dino, to see if it works," he overheard Kash say.

"What?" Darius responded. "I mean, why not have one of the BRADs do it?"

"Because I'm still not sure you're worth keeping around," Kash said. "So you can either impress me . . . or things are gonna go very bad for you. Very, very bad."

Ben's stomach sank.

"Okayyy," Darius said. "Which dinosaur?"

Ben was sure he heard Kash say, "Spinosaurus."

"If you're lucky, you can catch her while she's sleeping," Kash said. "That thing does *not* like BRADs. Or people."

Kash whacked another golf ball, then turned to face a BRAD-X. "He injects the dino with the chip, or . . . he doesn't come back. Got it?"

Ben noticed the BRAD-X's eye glow red. He was sure

the look of fear on his face matched the one on Darius's.

"Here goes nothing," Brooklynn said, pressing a button. Sparks flew out of the BRAD-X's control panel! Brooklynn tried to contain them, but it was like a shower of fireworks now! The BRAD-X shorted out as smoke poured forth. Brooklynn sighed.

"I can't do this," Darius said, trudging across the desert sand, holding the hypodermic in his hand.

The BRAD-X was right behind him, watching Darius's every move. He knew that Kash was serious. If he didn't do as he was told, the robot would end him.

Unless . . . unless, Darius thought, *the Spinosaurus ended the BRAD-X first!*

Darius saw the sleeping Spinosaurus up ahead, behind a huge rock formation. The dinosaur was simply immense.

Even though he moved quietly, the dinosaur seemed to sense him—maybe it had caught a whiff of his scent? At once, the Spinosaurus woke up, snarling, showing off rows of dangerously sharp teeth. Then it whipped its head around as Darius ducked behind a boulder.

Brooklynn had moved on to a new BRAD-X. With the panel open, Brooklynn held two wires in her hand. She suggested to Sammy, "Maybe you should stand back."

Touching the wires together, Brooklynn watched and waited. Nothing happened. So she did it again. *Still* nothing happened. And again. Nothing. One more try, and suddenly, the robot's eyes turned white!

Before Brooklynn and Sammy could react, the BRAD-X's head began to spin around, firing multiple shock orbs in rapid succession, one after the other! But Kenji and Yasmina pulled them away and out of sight. The shock orbs missed, until at last, the BRAD-X collapsed to the floor.

"I hate to pile on more bad news," Ben said, rushing over. "But Kash is making Darius inject a Spino with his new control chip! And if he doesn't do it, the BRAD-X has orders to. . . ."

Ben couldn't say the words. He didn't have to. Everyone knew what would happen.

Kenji faced Brooklynn. "B., we gotta switch it out. Like, *now.* How close are you?"

Everyone looked at Brooklynn like she had all the answers and knew what to do. She was Brooklynn—she could do anything, right?

But Brooklynn couldn't take that pressure. She

hurled a screwdriver down on the floor. "I can't do this, okay?! I just can't! I'm so sorry."

Kenji stepped in front of her. "No. *We're* sorry for putting so much pressure on you."

"And for thinking that hacking a robot would be easy," Sammy added.

"I didn't," Ben teased. "I assumed that's why we made Brooklynn do it."

That made Brooklynn smile. She didn't have to pretend to be someone she wasn't around her friends. She could just be herself.

"I've tried almost every BRAD-X in here," Brooklynn said. Then her eyes lit up. "But not every *BRAD*!"

Darius wanted to run, but he knew he wouldn't be able to get away from his "babysitter." And then there was the Spinosaurus to contend with.

The Spinosaurus lowered its head, barely noticing the robot. Instead, it focused on something behind the rocks—Darius. The Spinosaurus growled.

Darius had no choice. As he sprinted away from the dinosaur, the BRAD-X said, "Unauthorized security breach!"

The robot fired a series of shock orbs, and one of them clipped Darius's arm! But he kept running—from shock orbs and the Spinosaurus.

The kids overpowered the repair BRAD. Brooklynn popped open the control panel and snipped some wires inside.

"Hypothetically," Brooklynn said as she went to work, "the older model should be easier to hack, and we know it can send commands, so—"

"We can get this BRAD to command Darius's BRAD-X to listen to Darius!" Kenji said, figuring it out.

"That's genius!" Ben exclaimed.

"I just hope Darius can hang in there a little bit longer," Brooklynn said.

The Spinosaurus was rapidly closing the ground between it and Darius. Darius realized that he wouldn't be able to outrun the dinosaur. He knew he had to come up with some other plan.

That's when he saw the canister on the ground, among a bunch of broken BRAD parts!

Darius fumbled with the canister as the Spinosaurus came closer. The creature was nearly upon him when Darius managed to unleash the sleeping gas!

Heaving a sigh of relief, Darius was just about to move when, suddenly, the Spinosaurus burst out from the cloud of sleeping gas. Darius leaped back just as the dinosaur succumbed to the effects of the vapor. It fell down on top of Darius, knocking him out.

Brooklynn was in her zone now as she finished up her work on the repair BRAD. Kenji watched her at work—and all he could think was *She is awesome.* Just as Brooklynn closed the control panel, Yasmina raced over to her, carrying Dr. Turner's tablet.

It was exactly what she needed. Now she just had to save Darius!

Darius had no idea how long he had been asleep. He opened his eyes and crawled out from under the still-sleeping Spinosaurus, only to see the BRAD-X, which held out a claw. *Was it trying to help him up?* Focusing his eyes, Darius saw that the robot wasn't trying to help. It was holding the hypodermic. With a look of disgust, he grabbed the hypodermic and stared at the unconscious Spinosaurus.

Darius faced an impossible choice. Inject the chip into the innocent dinosaur so Kash could take control of the beast, or refuse and face the wrath of BRAD-X.

The robot seemed to sense the hesitation and

nudged Darius. The boy walked over to the sleeping dinosaur, his hands shaking. Hating himself, he placed the hypodermic at the base of the Spinosaurus' skull, and . . .

"Stop! You don't have to do this!"

Darius whirled around, surprised that it was the BRAD-X talking to him!

"I don't?"

"It's Brooklynn!" the BRAD-X said. "Long story short, I hacked a BRAD! Destroy the chip, and I'll have this guy tell Kash you injected the Spino with it. He'll never know."

With relish, Darius fired the chip into the sand and stomped on it.

"I can't control its weapons or anything yet," Brooklynn said. "So it's still going to be dangerous for you. But you are *so not* alone, dude."

For a moment, Darius was sure he was going to cry. "Thanks, guys," he said, then, in an urgent voice, "Hey, I know what Kash is up to! He's working on a big demonstration for Mantah Corp. investors. It's going down in six days. If we can figure out a way to mess it up . . ."

Brooklynn watched as the tablet electronically relayed Darius's message as a line of text: WE COULD PUT AN

END TO KASH'S DINO FIGHTS AND TAKE MANTAH CORP. DOWN FOR GOOD!

She was tired beyond tired, but she felt good. She had done it!

"That was amazing," Kenji said. "I mean, you're always amazing, but today was especially clutch."

"Thanks, Kenj," Brooklynn said with a smile. "That's really sweet."

"Too bad you can't post 'Unboxing a BRAD' when you get home," Kenji said nervously. "I bet your followers might like seeing the real you, mess-ups and all."

"Maybe you're right. And if I don't get any likes, so be it."

"Well, I like you," Kenji said suddenly.

At once, Brooklynn's eyes met Kenji's.

"I like *it.* The video," Kenji quickly corrected himself. "Not you. Well, you because you're in it. . . ."

Brooklyn nodded and turned away. Kenji breathed a sigh of relief.

In Kash's office, Darius handed over the hypodermic.

"Gotta admit," Kash said, "I'm impressed. Putting a chip in a Spino's noggin is not easy."

"Guess I got lucky," Darius replied. "Turns out the Spino was asleep *after* all."

Smiling, Kash pulled up an image of the Spinosaurus on the computer. An error message apeared that said **CHIP STATUS: FAILED.**

"Then why isn't it working?!" Kash screamed.

He glared at Darius, then directed his attention to the BRAD-X that had accompanied the boy.

"Task completed as directed," the BRAD-X intoned.

Biting his lip, Kash looked back at the computer and typed as fast as he could. A moment later, an image of Big Eatie popped up, along with an image of Pierce. Beneath them was another error message: **CHIP FAILURE.**

"Huh," Kash said. "Didn't work on the other two test subjects, either. All the dinos we chipped today are adults, so . . . their fully formed prefrontal cortexes are probably rejecting the control."

Darius felt relief wash over his body.

"Which means I'll need to use the chips on more . . . *impressionable* assets."

Relief turned to horror as Darius saw an image of a baby Brachiosaurus fill the screen.

"Odds are the chips will be too much and fry their little brains, but, hey, such is the price of genius," Kash said with callous glee.

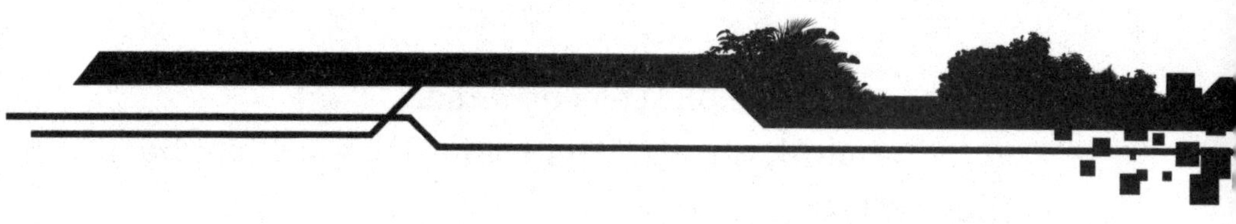

CHAPTER EIGHT

A few hours later, with Darius's BRAD-X now hacked and Kash asleep, the kids snuck into the compound. Getting past the Raptors wasn't so easy, but they managed to climb a rope attached to Darius's robot on the rooftop. Once they were inside with Darius, they headed for the elevator.

"This'll take you down to the med bay," Darius said as he and the BRAD-X hung back. "There's a nursery next to it. He's testing the control chips on the baby dinos first thing in the morning. Message me on the BRAD-X as soon as you get the babies out."

The elevator doors closed as Darius heard a voice behind him. "What are you doing out here?"

Darius turned around to see a sleepy Kash with his own robot. Thinking fast, Darius said, "I went up to the roof to get some air."

But Kash didn't want to hear Darius talk. He glared at the robot. "Where did the kid go?"

"The roof," the BRAD-X answered.

"Uh-huh," Kash said. "And was he doing anything he shouldn't have been?"

"Negative."

Kash yawned. "Escort him back to his room and make sure he stays here."

He started toward the elevator, nodding at his own BRAD. "Bring my cold brew downstairs to the nursery. Since the kid woke me up, might as well get some work done."

Darius's heart sank.

"Please don't make me go back to my room," Darius said. "I'm so bored! Can I play a video game or something? I thought I heard you playing one yesterday. I'll bet you have tons of sick games."

Kash raised an eyebrow. "You're a gamer?"

Sensing an opening, Darius pounced. "Yeah, it's sorta my thing back home. In fact, that's how I won my trip to Jurassic World. I'm kinda . . . awesome."

"Doubtful," Kash said as the elevator doors opened.

He wasn't sure if Kash would swallow the bait, so Darius decided to sweeten the deal. "That's cool. Most of my friends were scared to play me, too."

"Who said I was scared, loser?" Kash replied. "Fine. Schooling you seems like a good way to de-stress before I get to work."

Kash headed back to his office, and a relieved Darius followed.

The kids entered the vast med bay, unsure where to go. Airlock doors branched off from the main area. So they split up, each checking out a different airlock.

On her way, Sammy passed by unmarked double doors with no windows and no handles.

THUMP!

A startled Sammy jumped back. There was another loud THUMP and growling from behind the door.

"Hey, guys?" Ben said. "I think I found it!"

Sammy pulled herself away from the doors and caught up with Ben. He stood in front of a digital map, pointing to three blinking lights next to a baby dinosaur icon.

"See that?" Ben said. "Looks like there's only three baby dinos in the nursery."

Down the hall, they stopped at the first door they came to. There was a green light above the door, and a digital screen.

Ben looked at the screen and read. "Baby Brachiosaurus. Two months old. DNA extracted from Isla Sorna." Then he looked at his friends and said, "Won't take me long. Where we meeting after?"

"Medical bay," Brooklynn said. "We'll load 'em up on a platform and figure out which biome to take them to later."

Then Ben opened the door and headed inside.

The others walked to the next door with a green light. Brooklynn and Yasmina took that one.

Sammy had already reached the next door as Kenji read the screen. "Huh? Sinoceratops and Spinosaurus."

Sammy felt a sinking feeling in her stomach, and she said, "It's . . . a hybrid."

"What's everyone's obsession with making hybrids? Says the Sinoceratops DNA was 'extracted from live specimen on Isla Nublar.' Weird. How'd they get that?"

Inside the room, Sammy saw a plastic container on a desk. There was a cotton swab inside the container. One look, and Sammy knew *exactly* where they got the DNA. Back on Isla Nublar, before the group had bonded, before she had revealed her dealings with Mantah Corp., Sammy had taken a DNA swab from a Sinoceratops.

Racing over to the dinosaur pen, she saw a three-foot tall baby dinosaur with the body and frill of a Sinoceratops and sail of a Spinosaurus.

"Whoa," Kenji said, looking at an incubation chamber full of eggs. "Looks like they got more of these cooking."

"I'm so sorry," a guilt-ridden Sammy whispered.

"The Jurassic World video game," Darius said. He stood

in front of a huge screen in Kash's office, holding a controller. Kash was right next to him, holding another.

"Gotta say, there's something funny about playing a game where we run from dinosaurs, when—ya know—we're on an island filled with dinosaurs," Darius continued.

"Eh, I prefer this way," Kash said. "I can eat nachos while I own these punk lizards."

"No, totally. I love *punking* dinosaurs. It's probably why I'm so unbeatable at this game."

"We'll see about that," Kash said as Darius selected TWO-PLAYER RACE from the menu.

"All right, champ," Ben said. "Your buddy Ben is here to save you."

With a handful of berries, he approached the crate where the baby Brachiosaurus slept. He placed the berries beneath the dinosaur's nose, patting the creature.

Slowly, the dinosaur opened her eyes. One look at the hand on her face and she startled, knocking Ben down!

Berries flew everywhere as the baby dinosaur zipped around the room.

Yasmina and Brooklynn took some sticks and leaves from a nest in the corner of the room and approached the dinosaur. This was also a Sinoceratops-Spinosaurus hybrid, but it was a light blue-gray.

"Move, baby," Yasmina said, holding out a branch. "You gotta get outta here. Especially since it's so cold in here."

But the dinosaur refused to move. Taking the stick from Yasmina, Brooklynn offered it to the baby.

"Okay, widdle one," Brooklynn said in a cutesy voice. "Auntie Yaz and Big Sister Brooky are here."

The dinosaur just stared at Brooklynn, tilting its head to one side.

"Wanna go for a walky-poo?" Brooklynn asked, using her cutesy voice. "I pwomise, it's someplace weally, weally special!"

The voice seemed to work. The baby followed Brooklynn!

Yasmina laughed. "There's a ninety-five percent chance I'm gonna make you do that voice for Sam, Ben, and Kenj later."

"Not Kenji!" Brooklynn gasped.

Yasmina gave Brooklynn a look and wouldn't stop staring. At last, Brooklynn rolled her eyes and said, "Kenji said he likes me, okay?"

But Brooklynn wasn't sure if Kenji really meant it. If they liked each other, would it ruin their friendship? She wasn't sure. . . .

"You poor thing," Sammy said as she watched the baby Sino-Spino eat a slab of meat. The dino snapped at her. "Probably cranky. I don't blame you. Must be hard, stuck here, not knowing who to trust—"

"We gotta move," Kenji said. "Now."

But Sammy wasn't paying attention. She crouched down, getting even closer to the baby dinosaur.

Then he tried to move the dinosaur. The Sino-Spino growled, snapping at Kenji.

"Kenji! Look what you did!" Sammy said, scolding her friend. She put down another slab of meat. "We'll move when you're ready. Not when mean old Kenji says so."

"What happened to Sammy 'the littlest ones need the firmest hand' Gutierrez?" Kenji teased.

Sammy gestured at the white dinosaur with big eyes. "I just . . . This poor little angel. Angel! That's what we'll call her." Kenji tried to pet Angel, but the dinosaur nipped his finger!

"Ugh!" Kash shouted, slamming his controller down.

Darius smiled. "It's okay, dude. You haven't had as much experience running from dinosaurs as I have."

Kash gritted his teeth and put the controller down. Then he turned to look at the BRAD-X and sneered, "I'm over this. Take him to his room. I'm heading downstairs."

Darius knew he had to keep Kash occupied.

"How about a rematch?" Darius asked. "Come on, I'll take it easier on you this time."

Kash turned red in the face. "Are you—?! I wasn't even trying. I just have work to do. Actual, important work."

"Whatevs." Darius shrugged. "Just sounds like someone hates to lose."

Seething, Kash stomped back over to Darius. The boy thought he had pushed it too far, but Kash just walked over to his computer and started to type.

"Lemme just do this one quick thing . . . then it's game time for real."

No matter what Ben did, the Brachiosaurus just wanted to run around and butt Ben. Berries didn't seem to interest the dinosaur.

He took a deep breath, walking away. The Brachiosaurus rammed right into him again! Then the baby slapped him with her tail. The dinosaur bellowed and nuzzled Ben.

"Wait . . . you just wanna play?" Ben said, getting it.

"Bumpy was all about the berries, but I guess you're not Bumpy. All right. Let's try it your way."

"That's not even—did you mess with the game?" Darius asked. He couldn't believe what had just happened. In the game, his avatar dove into a gyrosphere to evade the jaws of a Velociraptor. But then suddenly, the gyrosphere's door opened, and the Raptor went inside and devoured his avatar! Then it was GAME OVER.

"Don't know what you're talking about," Kash said, doing his best to look innocent. "Sounds like *someone* hates to lose."

Darius huffed, frustrated.

"Best three out of five?" Kash said with a grin.

While Kenji struggled to get Angel out the door, Brooklynn and Yasmina already had their little one out in the hallway. Then they bumped right into Kenji, who looked exhausted—but he had succeeded in getting Angel into the hallway, too. She rammed right into Brooklynn and Yasmina's dinosaur! At once, they began to play.

"*Awww,* look at 'em," Brooklynn said. "They must be siblings!"

"It's cute until we get caught," Kenji reminded her. "If we're gonna keep moving, we need to separate them."

The kids decided to switch things up, so Yasmina and Sammy took Angel, while Brooklynn and Kenji went ahead with the other dinosaur to the center of the med bay.

Yasmina and Sammy watched as Brooklynn and Kenji headed off with their dinosaur. Then Angel plopped down in the middle of the hallway.

"Okay, Sammy," Yasmina said. "Do your animal thing."

"Aww, give her a minute. She just needs some love. I bet all she's ever gotten in her whole little life is a cold, uncaring BRAD claw."

Yasmina sensed something was up. "What's the deal? Sammy?"

Sammy was quiet, then replied, "Angel's here because of me. And so is her brother. They were made from the samples I stole from Nublar. They've spent their whole lives down here, no sunlight, no fresh air, all because of me."

Yasmina put a hand on her friend's shoulder. "You may have taken the sample—under threat, by the way—but it's Mantah Corp.'s fault for doing all this to the animals. Coddling Angel isn't going to help her. But getting her out of here, saving her from Kash, *that* will."

Sammy smiled, realizing that Yasmina was right. Before they could do anything, Ben turned the corner.

He was being chased by the baby Brachiosaurus.

"It's the only way to get her to move!" Ben explained.

Sammy then turned to Angel, determined. She whistled and stamped her feet on the ground. "Now, you listen to me. I'm sorry you had it rough, but if you ever want a better life, you are gonna move!"

A moment later, Angel started moving.

Brooklynn realized they would need to cover their tracks so it looked like the baby dinosaurs had escaped on their own. Kenji saw a fuse box and suggested they just blow a fuse.

Ben entered with the Brachiosaurus, followed by Sammy, Yasmina, and Angel.

Kenji examined the fuse box and unscrewed a knob. The lights flickered, and the doors of the nursery creaked and shorted out.

"There we go!" Kenji said.

But the Brachiosaurus and the Sino-Spinos suddenly began to play, bumping into one another. In their exuberance, one of them smashed a fuse box! There was an ominous buzz as all the lights turned off and all the doors shorted out. Suddenly, another pair of doors opened. They were the doors that Sammy had passed by before . . . where she heard a decidedly unfriendly but not unfamiliar sound.

Heavy footsteps thundered in the dark as a Ceratosaurus stomped out. The creature stood between them and the platform to the surface!

Darius glared at the out-of-place dancing T. rex in the video game and then at Kash. "A dance break?" he protested. "Are you kidding me? How is there even a cheat code for that?"

Kash chuckled. "Don't make excuses for your failures, kid. Just like, *be better.*"

Before he could say anything else, a beeping sound came from his tablet.

"Power outage in the med bay," Kash said, leaving the room.

"Wait!" Darius called out as Kash headed for the elevator. "I gotta know how you hacked the game like that!"

"Earned a new respect for me, eh?" Kash said.

Darius nodded. Anything to keep Kash occupied and away from the med bay until his friends had a chance to get away.

"Yeah, I thought I was good, but it was like you taught me *the game* how it was supposed to be played. Show me how?"

Kash thought for a second. "Nah. Maybe later. I gotta check things out down there."

He was almost at the elevator when he noticed that

Darius was right behind him. "Where do you think you're going?"

"How am I supposed to 'be better' if I'm not learning from the best?"

"Fine," Kash said. "But keep to yourself and don't be annoying." When the elevator arrived in the med bay, Kash pushed right past Darius. The room was cast in darkness, and from what Darius could tell, everything was a mess.

"Out of my way," Kash said.

"I'm not sure if—"

There was a fierce snarl as the Ceratosaurus jumped out from the shadows! Kash stumbled past Darius back to the elevator.

Darius saw no sign of his friends. Acting on instinct, Darius dashed back into the elevator and just made it inside as the dinosaur reached the elevator and the doors shut. The Ceratosaurus slammed the car, sending the occupants crashing to the floor. Kash cowered behind Darius.

"That was close," Sammy said.

She stood on the platform with Yasmina and Ben, along with Angel and the Brachiosaurus. They had been separated from Brooklynn and Kenji while evading the Ceratosaurus and were now in the forest biome.

The Brachiosaurus galloped away from the platform and into the forest.

"Hey! Hold on, girl!" Ben cried. "Wait!"

Sammy and Yasmina smiled as they watched Angel slowly wander off, grazing in the grass.

"She's safe," Yasmina said. "Thanks to you."

"Thanks to us," Sammy replied with a smile.

In the arctic biome, the platform rose, and Brooklynn and Kenji shivered.

"Let's get out of here, fast," Brooklynn suggested.

Kenji couldn't help grinning at the little blue dinosaur with pale off-white highlights as it played in the snow. It might have been the first time the creature had ever been outside.

Kenji chased after the dinosaur, playing with him.

"Hey, did we name the little guy? How about . . . Rebel?"

"I like it!" Brooklynn said. Then a realization dawned on her. What she really meant was, she liked Kenji.

When the elevator doors opened in the med bay the next time, the Ceratosaurus was fast asleep on the cold floor. A cloud of sleeping gas hung around the dinosaur.

Darius and Kash covered their faces as the gas began to dissipate. The room was destroyed. Kash shook his head, flustered. "How did this happen?"

Darius knew how it had happened, of course, but he kept his mouth shut.

Kash headed for the nursery. He emerged a moment later, frowning.

"They're gone," he said. "Did you do this?"

"I was with you the whole time," Darius said, shaking his head.

CHAPTER NINE

"What are the odds that every single fuse blows, opening *all* the dinosaur pens the night before I need them?" Kash fumed.

"Well," Darius began. "Maybe they—"

"Ugh!" Kash grunted. "I had a whole plan. The boss shows up and is met by baby dinosaurs who do whatever he tells them to and then BOOM! He makes me his partner. Before he knows it, I—"

Kash must have realized he was babbling, because he stopped and stared at Darius. Then he groaned in a rage and shrieked, "WHERE THE HECK DID THOSE THINGS GO?!"

"Maybe the Ceratosaurus ate them?" Darius offered.

"Yeah? And did he mop the floors after, too? There was no trace of anything. We need to sweep the biomes."

"Shouldn't we check down here first? I mean, it's

not like baby dinosaurs can work an elevator," Darius pointed out.

For a moment, Darius thought Kash was going to scream at him. Then, calmly, the man looked at a robot and said, "Check the entire underground facility."

Two BRAD-Xs obeyed and went off to search.

"Where are the other new BRADs?" Kash asked.

"The BRAD-X units are acclimatizing the new assets," a robot said.

"We don't have time for that," Kash said. "Just put the *new* assets somewhere and find the *missing* assets. Now!"

"Affirmative," the robot said before leaving the room.

"It's not feeding time," Kash said as he noticed one of the feeding platforms was raised. "When was this platform last used?"

"Searching records," a BRAD-X said. "Platform use was unauthorized."

"Guess they *can* use elevators," Kash said, glaring at Darius.

Darius had done everything he could to buy time for his friends, but he couldn't stall any longer. He could only hope that they had managed to get somewhere safe.

"I want every BRAD searching the biomes for those baby dinosaurs!" Kash screamed, his whole body trembling.

"Affirmative," a robot replied. Its eye turned red. Seconds later in the warehouse, the eyes of a group of BRAD-Xs also lit up the same ominous red.

Sammy and Yasmina sat with Angel beneath a tree and watched the dinosaur munch happily on a berry bush. Ben soon joined them, his arms full of berries for the little Brachiosaurus who still hadn't been named. Except there *was* no little Brachiosaurus.

"Where is the other one?" Ben asked.

Yasmina looked around, but she saw no trace of the dinosaur. "We thought she was with you."

They were interrupted by Sammy, who gasped loudly and pointed at the airlock. A swarm of BRAD-Xs entered the biome, their green scanning lights sweeping the area. Ben sprinted off to find the baby Brachiosaurus before it was too late.

"Get Angel somewhere safe," Ben said as he got up to go. The girls nodded and made for the cave.

As Ben pumped his legs, he saw a BRAD-X approaching the Brachiosaurus in the distance! The dinosaur ran around, zigzagging playfully.

Ben grabbed a rock and hurled it at the robot. The

BRAD-X turned around and fired shock orbs in Ben's direction! Ben dove behind a tree and held his breath as he watched the robot scan the area. He saw another BRAD-X heading for the Brachiosaurus. He gasped. The little dinosaur was now completely surrounded by robots.

"Sorry," he whispered. "I should've been there for you."

The BRAD-Xs weren't hurting the Brachiosaurus, Ben noticed, but they were herding the dinosaur into the jungle biome.

Ben figured they were taking her to Kash's compound. He had sworn that after Bumpy, he wouldn't get close to another dinosaur, not like that. And yet, here he was. Ben followed.

At the compound, the BRAD-Xs stood around the Brachiosaurus. One robot grabbed the dinosaur and kept her still.

Darius and his hacked BRAD stood next to Kash. When he was sure that Kash wasn't looking, Darius removed the chip from the hypodermic he was holding.

Kash held out his hand and said, "Gimme the injector."

Darius gave it to him, minus the chip, as Kash narrowed his eyes.

Gazing at the hypodermic, Kash said, "Where . . . Swear I put a chip in here already."

As Kash took another chip from his pocket, Darius felt his heart sink.

The man walked toward the Brachiosaurus with the loaded hypodermic.

Ben was hiding now, and he was close enough to see exactly what was going on. The Brachiosaurus squirmed, trying to evade Kash, but it was no use.

"Stay still!" Kash shouted as he eyed the base of the dinosaur's skull.

Darius heard the hypodermic.

"Nailed it!" Kash said. "Or rather, chipped it!"

Chuckling to himself, Kash looked over at Darius, who forced himself to smile. Then Kash ordered the BRAD-Xs away, and the Brachiosaurus ran off.

"And . . . ," Kash said expectantly, taking the tablet from Darius. He hit a STOP button on the screen.

Suddenly, the Brachiosaurus stopped running. Ben could see the baby dinosaur tense her muscles, straining, trying to run, but it was no use.

Kash smiled.

Darius was disgusted.

Kash noticed.

"What's wrong with you?" he asked.

"I think I ate something weird," Darius said, attempting to cover. "Um, gotta go—"

Then he ran, his BRAD-X following him.

"If you make a mess, you're cleaning it up!" Kash shouted.

Meanwhile, Ben watched helplessly as the Brachiosaurus continued to struggle. His eyes filling with tears, Ben began to breathe heavily.

"Didn't want to get too close again, huh?" he said, remembering Bumpy. "Wanted to protect your own heart!"

He managed to get his breathing under control, then looked at the Brachiosaurus once more. Their eyes locked, and Ben felt the creature's utter panic.

"And now you've lost them both," Ben muttered as he slammed a fist against a tree.

Sammy and Yasmina had almost reached the cave. They continued feeding berries to Angel, which seemed to keep the dinosaur moving.

The girls heard a mew and saw Brooklynn and Kenji as they approached from the other side of the cave with their playful dinosaur.

Then, from out of nowhere, Ben appeared, panting.

"No time to talk!" he shouted. "Get inside, now!"

Once inside, Ben wouldn't stop pacing as the kids and Dr. Turner watched.

"Kash did it," he said. "With the chips . . . he got her, and now he's controlling her. She tried to fight it, but she . . . she couldn't. She wasn't strong enough."

Ben looked at the bandaged doctor and said, "Enough is enough. We have to take Kash down."

Darius watched as the Brachiosaurus tried to escape. A frustrated Kash pressed button after button on his tablet.

"Jump. Jump!" Kash shouted. "Lay down. Sit. Fine, stop!"

Kash smashed a button, and the Brachiosaurus froze in place.

Noticing Darius had come back, Kash said, "Only command the thing follows is 'stop.' I'm gonna see if I can't amp up the frequency. It's either gonna do what I want, or its little head will explode. Either way, we're seeing something cool today."

Then he looked at Darius.

"You hurl?"

Darius gave an embarrassed look as Kash laughed and went inside the compound. He stayed outside, his heart breaking as he looked at the helpless dinosaur.

"We're gonna get you out of this," Darius said softly. "Just gotta be brave a little bit longer."

Back at the cave, the kids tried to get their dinosaurs under control. At least, Kenji and Brooklynn tried. Sammy and Yasmina already seemed to have figured out the best way to secure Angel's cooperation: berries, and plenty of them.

Kenji tried petting Rebel to calm him down, and then he hit the QUIET button on the tablet, making a dinosaur sound.

"Quiet, buddy," Kenji said. "You can do this. Shhhhh."

Brooklynn was impressed with how Kenji was taking care of Rebel. He really was trying to be a good dinosaur dad . . . and then she thought about Kenji's own father and wondered if their strained relationship might have something to do with it.

She helped Kenji as Ben walked over. "Darius is on board with the plan," he said. They had contacted him via the hacked BRAD-X.

"So what's the next step of the plan, Ben?" Brooklynn asked.

"Well, after the Sino-Spinos lure Kash to the waterfall cave . . . I hit that sucker with a surprise shot of knockout gas. Well, technically, Darius's BRAD will, once I activate it from the tablet, but you know what I mean. And then we lock Kash inside. Done."

"Kash! Come quick!" Darius hollered. He saw Yasmina in the trees nearby. That meant it was time to put their plan into operation.

Kash ran out of the compound with a BRAD, looking annoyed.

"What?!" Kash demanded.

"Look!" Darius said, pointing at the spot in the jungle where Yasmina was.

Kash stared blankly as Angel suddenly came running from the jungle, heading for an airlock.

"That little . . . ," Kash grumbled as he pulled up the Brachiosaurus on his tablet.

"Take this thing back and put it in the nursery," he said to his BRAD. Then he looked at Darius and said, "Come on!"

Kash took off after the baby Sino-Spino. Darius followed Kash, his own BRAD-X right there with him.

"Okay," Darius said so the BRAD-X could hear it. "He took the bait."

Not far away, Sammy offered some berries to Angel, and the dinosaur ran right to her! She gave Angel a berry and pulled her deep into a shrub.

The two hid together, and Sammy saw Kash arrive with Darius. Kash looked around but couldn't see anything. "Where'd it go?!"

Darius pointed at the open airlock and entered. Kash seemed suspicious, but he followed Darius anyway.

"Okay," Ben said, holding the tablet. He was still in the forest biome with Brooklynn, Kenji, and Rebel. "Darius will be here any minute with Kash."

Then he tucked the tablet under his arm and said, "Let's move."

But before they could depart, they were interrupted by a screeching sound from above.

"Pteranodons," Ben said with fear in his voice. "Why'd it have to be Pteranodons?!"

A Pteranodon plunged from the sky, heading for Rebel. The dinosaur yelped loudly and ran off, heading toward the airlock. The flying reptile followed, trying to snatch Rebel.

Brooklynn and Kenji ran after the baby dinosaur. Ben tightened his grip on the tablet. He froze in his tracks at the sight of another Pteranodon. Ben sprinted in the opposite direction as the Pteranodon plunged toward him!

Ben rolled out of the way, got up, and kept running. A Pteranodon came for him, screeching, and Ben flung his arm holding the tablet at it, trying to keep the creature at bay. It snatched the tablet away from him and soared into the sky!

Kash entered the forest biome with Darius and his hacked BRAD-X. A glob of dino poop almost hit Kash, and when he looked up, a Pteranodon swooped down! Kash leapt back.

"Wait," Darius said. "The 'new assets' were Pteranodons?"

"Yeah, and those BRADs just let them loose!" Kash complained.

"You told them to put them wherever!" Darius said, irritated.

"That's obviously not what I meant," Kash snarled as he headed back to the airlock in the direction of the jungle biome.

Darius didn't know what to do. This wasn't the plan at all! So he followed Kash and said, "Uh, what about the baby dinos?"

"Chill, kid," Kash said. "I'm not getting eaten by a flying lizard to find them."

"He's gonna get caught!" Brooklynn screamed. She and

Kenji raced through the forest. "Kenji, do something!"

Pursuing the Pteranodon that was following Rebel, they headed right for the biome wall!

Kenji caught up to the dinosaur, jumped atop him, and directed him to a hiding spot. Brooklynn joined them a second later.

Thinking fast, Kenji did his best to mimic a sound from the tablet. It worked! Rebel suddenly became quiet, despite the Pteranodon overhead. Losing sight of its prey, the Pteranodon looked all around for another potential meal—but slammed right into the wall of the biome and spiraled to the ground.

"I can't believe that worked," Kenji said. Then he looked at Rebel. "I am *so* proud of you!"

A second later, Brooklynn hugged Kenji close and said, "I'm so proud of *you.*"

Kenji couldn't believe what he was about to do. "Brooklynn," he said, "listen. This is so not the time, but I really—"

"Me too!" Brooklynn interjected.

"You do?"

Brooklynn nodded, and they smiled. At last, each knew that they liked the other.

"We need to get back," she said. "We might still be able to lead Kash to the waterfall."

Elsewhere in the forest biome, Ben ran after the Pteranodon that had taken the tablet.

"You got this," Ben said to himself. "Sure, Pteranodons ripped you out of a speeding monorail and dropped you like yesterday's garbage over a predator-filled jungle. Is that any reason to be afraid of them now?"

Then he got a good look at the Pteranodons flying all around him, and he hid.

"Yes," he said to himself. "Yes, it is."

A moment later, he caught sight of the Pteranodon with the tablet. It was walking in front of him. Summoning all his courage, Ben let out a battle cry and leaped at the Pteranodon! The creature flew off, but Ben gave chase. The Pteranodon dipped, and Ben jumped up and grabbed the tablet!

Which was great, except for the fact that the Pteranodon didn't let go. Now Ben was being taken away by the flying reptile!

"Don't look down!" Ben muttered as he dangled from the tablet the Pteranodon held in its beak. Down below, he saw a stream, and that gave him an idea. Ben hammered away at the Pteranodon's beak. Opening its mouth, the dinosaur let go of the tablet and, in the process, Ben.

Ben fell into the stream with a SPLASH! Recovering quickly, he checked the screen—no sign of any cracks.

He pressed a button, and the device turned on.

"Yes!" he shouted.

The sound attracted the Pteranodon, and it swooped down, heading for Ben.

Ben threw his arms over his head, but nothing happened. He looked up when he heard a whirring sound, only to see four drones above. They surrounded the Pteranodon, keeping the creature at bay.

Ben sighed and ran back to Dr. Turner's cave.

In the waterfall cave, Brooklynn and Kenji huddled with Rebel, who continued to mew loudly. Nearby, Kash pointed in the direction of the sound.

"Look!" Darius said, and Kash ran with Darius right behind him.

"Quiet," Kenji said, making the soft dinosaur sound for "quiet." Rebel stopped making sounds.

Ben hid in the trees as Kash and Darius approached.

"Where'd it go?" Kash exclaimed. Darius kept pace, his own BRAD-X following. The robot moved ahead, drawing nearer to Kash.

Ben looked down at the tablet. "Just a bit closer," he said, waiting to hit the sleeping gas button.

Scanning the area for any sign of the baby dinosaur, Kash grunted. Finally, he stopped walking, and the

BRAD-X was right in front of him.

"Time to go night night, Kash," Ben said, and he hit the button.

Nothing happened. Ben hit the button again. And again. And again.

Darius heard a click from the BRAD-X, like it was trying to do something but couldn't.

"Where's the sleeping gas?" Ben said, panicking. He eyed Darius as if to say, "What should I do?" Thinking quickly, he dashed to the cave.

"Why are you acting so weird?" Kash asked, noticing Darius staring at the robot.

Darius gulped, realizing that he would have to take matters into his own hands.

"Um," he said, taking a step closer. "I . . ."

Suddenly, the sound of a baby dinosaur growling came from inside the cave!

"Behind the waterfall!" Kash said.

"How the heck could that thing just wander in here?" Kash said. He was inside Dr. Turner's cave, looking for the source of the dinosaur sound.

It was really Ben in the kitchen, trying to keep out of sight. He heard Kash's footsteps coming toward him. Kash was just about to enter when a dinosaur bellowed from the bedroom. He went to the sleeping area.

"I'll look out here!" Darius said, unaware of Ben's location. "You check the back!"

Ben peeked out and saw that Kash was already in the sleeping area. He ran over to Darius, who looked at him as if to say, "Exactly what *is* the plan?!"

There was no dinosaur in the sleeping area, only the recorded *sound* of a dinosaur, playing on a tablet!

Kash realized what had happened, and he picked up the tablet. Angrily, he headed for the door as it slammed shut in his face!

"I had to leave the tablet," Ben explained as he and Darius stood on the other side of the door with the hacked BRAD-X.

"Um . . . ," Darius said, pointing at the door. Then he picked up a rock and smashed the virtual lock on the door.

Full of rage, Kash tried to slide the door open, but it was no use. He soon gave up, throwing the tablet against the door.

"You did it," Darius said.

"*We* did it," Ben corrected him. They high-fived and gave each other a massive hug.

They could hear Kash banging on the door, ranting,

"I'm gonna enjoy making you regret this!"

Back in the nursery, the Brachiosaurus sat in the corner as Ben approached.

"Listen," he said as the Brachiosaurus started knocking into him playfully. "I know I messed up. I tried to keep you at a distance so that neither of us would get hurt, but that didn't work so well, did it? I promise I'll never let anyone hurt you again."

The dinosaur looked up at Ben, and he smiled at her.

"You remind me of her," Ben said, thinking of Bumpy. "You got a lot of guts, kid. A lotta guts. And fire. Yeah, you're just a little firecracker, aren't ya?"

In the jungle cave, the others waited as Darius, Ben, and the Brachiosaurus entered.

"We got him!" Darius shouted. "Ben's plan worked!"

"Incredible," Dr. Turner said, admiration in her voice. Then she gave the Brachiosaurus a pat on the head. "You're *all* so incredible."

"Thanks, guys," Ben said. "That was for Firecracker . . . Bumpy . . . and Mae . . . and for everyone else that jerkface Kash mighta hurt in the future."

"I'm sorry, Firecracker?" Yasmina asked.

"Oh yeah," Ben said. "I named her."

For the first time in what seemed like forever, the group relaxed.

Isla Nublar. A jungle miles away. Bumpy emerged from the trees and stomped through what remained of Camp Cretaceous. She slowly walked to the place where Ben had once lived and mewled, calling out for her friend. When he didn't appear, she settled down for a nap as if to wait for him.

CHAPTER TEN

"Hey, I think something's wrong with Rebel," Brooklynn said. "He's chill, but not usually *this* chill."

The Sino-Spino was playing just a moment ago, but now it rolled over and yawned, like it was going to sleep. A sluggish Angel nipped at Sammy, missing her hand.

"Angel's acting weird, too," Sammy said. "She's usually more . . . bitey."

"No issues for Firecracker," Ben said as he chased after the Brachiosaurus. "She's right at home!"

"Maybe that's the problem," Sammy suggested. "Maybe they don't belong here in the jungle biome. But Sinoceratops live in the jungle. It doesn't make sense."

"Well, they're also half Spinosaurus, like the one in the desert biome. Maybe we should try there?"

"Works for me," Yasmina said.

The girls gathered the dinosaurs and headed for the desert biome.

"We're taking the kids to the desert!" Yasmina said,

passing Ben and Firecracker.

"Have fun!" Ben said.

He was just about to give Firecracker some berries when the dinosaur darted past him. He turned around and saw Dr. Turner holding a leafy branch. Firecracker ran over and started to eat.

"You did a good thing, Ben," the doctor said. "She's finally free."

Scratching Firecracker, he said, "We got her out of that cage, sure. But she's still got that control chip in her. If that tech gets into the wrong hands."

Dr. Turner knew exactly what he meant. "Then I guess we better get that chip out of her, huh?"

They headed for the med bay, leaving Darius and Kenji behind.

Brooklynn, Sammy, and Yasmina gave their dinosaurs a push, shoving them through the airlock. At last, the baby Sino-Spinos were in the desert biome. They looked around for any sign of the Spinosaurus, but there was none.

"Coast is clear," Brooklynn said.

The baby dinosaurs padded off into the desert, promptly collapsing beneath the shade of a tree, panting.

"Okay," Brooklynn mused, rolling her eyes. "So that's a no on the desert."

Both dinosaurs began to whine.

"Hey," Brooklynn suddenly realized. "When we were in the arctic, Rebel was super playful. Plus, look at them! They'd blend right in with snow and ice. That's gotta be where they belong! Sorry, guys. I should have thought of that sooner."

"To the arctic!" Yasmina shouted.

They tried pushing the dinosaurs toward the airlock, but both Angel and Rebel began to yelp.

The Spinosaurus suddenly appeared, roaring.

Realizing they would at least have to feed Kash, Darius and Kenji walked to the waterfall cave. But when they got there, something was wrong.

Like, *really* wrong. Kash was gone!

Kenji searched the kitchen area while Darius took the bedroom. Both returned, shaking their heads.

"How'd he get out?" Kenji wondered. "Where did he go?"

"I don't know," Darius said. "Probably back to his compound, or the med bay, or—"

"Ben and Mae!" they said.

Ben hugged Firecracker, trying to comfort the dinosaur.

Dr. Turner held up a pair of tweezers with a tiny chip in its grasp.

"Got it," she said.

Ben knelt in front of Firecracker, looking her in the eyes.

"Thanks, Mae," he said. "It's nice to be around an adult who loves dinosaurs as much as we do."

"We'll never make it," Brooklynn said.

The girls and the dinosaurs crouched down behind a small boulder in a desperate bid to hide. The Spinosaurus sniffed the shrubs. The dinosaur stood between them and the airlock.

One by one, they crept out from behind the rock. But once they left the shade, Rebel and Angel whined, and the noise drew the attention of the Spinosaurus.

"Run!" Yasmina shouted as the Spinosaurus charged.

Yasmina found the door. She opened it, and the girls pulled the dinosaurs through and slammed the keypad. The door closed on the Spinosaurus.

Darius and Kenji had made their way back to the jungle biome to search Kash's compound. Once they arrived, Kenji went down to the med bay to get Ben and

Dr. Turner, while Darius headed to Kash's office.

The lights automatically turned on when Darius entered the office. He heard footsteps coming down the hall! Hiding behind a couch, he saw Kash enter.

"Hot take, Boss," Kash said. "We just get rid of it."

Darius was shocked to see that Kash wasn't on the phone or talking to a BRAD. He was speaking with a real live human being! But Darius couldn't see who it was.

"Check it, Boss," Kash said. "We just get rid of the Kentro. It's injured and broke off a tail spike, so . . . it's not even that cool anymore."

The man sighed. "Always so shortsighted, Kash. It's no wonder you got outsmarted by a twelve-year-old child."

Darius watched as Kash grimaced, clearly upset at the thought.

"Waste not, want not," the man continued. "The assets in the new biome are devouring meat at an unprecedented rate. Let's see if two tons of Kentrosaurus will satiate their hunger."

"Oh man," Kash said, sounding frightened. "You released those things already? I, uh, haven't figured out a way to contain them. The drones don't work because of the—"

The man turned toward the door and walked away. "I'm aware. It doesn't matter, because we won't be here. The BRADs will take the Kentrosaurus there while you and I prepare the forest biome for the presentation."

"You got it, Daniel!" Kash said with forced enthusiasm.

Darius heard the door close and footsteps continue down the hallway. He stood up and raced over to the door. Then he heard footsteps coming back!

Diving behind the couch, he was surprised when he heard a voice say, "Dude, why are you hiding like that?"

It was Kenji!

"Aw, they look so at home!" Brooklynn said, watching Angel and Rebel bound through the snow in the arctic biome. Brooklynn, Sammy, and Yasmina sat in the snow glider.

"Okay," Yasmina said. "You guys ready to go?"

But neither Brooklynn nor Sammy were ready to leave the dinosaurs yet.

"Come on," Yasmina prodded. "We all know leaving them here is the best thing for them."

"Yeah," Brooklynn replied. "But it's still hard."

Yasmina gestured at Angel and Rebel. They continued to play in the snow.

"They aren't sad, so we shouldn't be, either," she said. "Now, come on." She took the controls, and the snow glider began to pull away.

"Yaz!" Sammy shouted. "What are you doing?"

"Giving you the push you need," Yasmina said.

But Brooklynn grabbed the controls, and they jerked back to the dinosaurs.

"We don't need a push, we just need a minute!" she said. "We aren't ready to say goodbye."

The two girls were now fighting over the snow glider controls as the vehicle veered from one side to the other.

The girls kept on struggling, and suddenly, the snow glider slammed into a snowbank.

Yasmina tried backing out, but it was useless.

"Kash's boss is here," Darius said, clutching two golf clubs in his hands as he and Kenji ran out of the compound.

Ben and Dr. Turner were waiting as Firecracker grazed on some ferns.

"He wants to kill Pierce!" Darius continued. "He's having the BRADs take her to a new biome with new assets. They're gonna use her as food!"

"There's a *new* biome?" Ben asked, surprised.

"It was under construction for a while," Dr. Turner said, "but they must have finished it. The airlock is just through those trees."

"You guys try to stop the BRADs, and Kenji and I will stop the new dinos," Darius said.

Darius tossed a golf club to Ben. He and Dr. Turner left the compound.

Then Kenji headed into the jungle with Darius right behind.

Thick fog rolled through the swamp, making it nearly impossible to see. Something rippled in the water as splashing sounds grew louder. Things with legs and tails made their way through the water until they reached a pile of raw meat. Jaws flashed and teeth were bared as the creatures devoured what had been set out for them. In seconds, the food was gone, and the dinosaurs scattered. There was nothing left behind.

Nothing.

The girls found the other snow glider and scrambled inside. They were just about head off for the airlock when they saw something emerge over the snowy landscape.

It was a BRAD-X! But not just any robot.

"That's Darius's BRAD-X!" Brooklynn shouted.

"Message delivery," the robot said. " 'The Kentrosaurus is in trouble. We need your help.' "

Concerned looks crossed their faces as Brooklynn looked at the BRAD-X. "Tell us where to go," she said.

Ben and Dr. Turner followed the three med BRADs as they took Pierce to a different airlock. On instinct, Ben charged a BRAD and knocked it to the floor with the golf club. Dr. Turner was already at Pierce's side, trying to comfort her friend.

"It's okay, Pierce," she said. "I'm here."

The sound of her voice immediately calmed the dinosaur.

More BRADs appeared. They shoved Pierce onto a platform. Ben tried to charge those robots, but Dr. Turner yanked him back.

"Ben! There's too many!"

He knew that Dr. Turner was right. The only choice he had was to step onto the platform with Dr. Turner and Pierce, along with the rest of the BRADs, which were surrounding them.

Darius and Kenji walked through the swamp, unable to see practically anything for the fog. They had raided a BRAD warehouse, grabbing some shock orbs just in case.

Something darted in front of them!

"Oh no," Darius said. "Dilophosaurus."

Kenji noted the fear in Darius's voice. "It didn't seem *that* scary."

"They spit poisonous venom," Darius replied.

"They do what now?" Kenji said, just as a Dilophosaurus jumped out right in front of them!

The boys screamed and turned to run. But two more Dilophosaurs blocked their path! Frills stuck out from around the dinosaurs' necks as venom shot from their mouths.

Darius and Kenji dodged the thick, gooey venom, and scrambling over tree roots and through puddles, they saw a platform opening. There was Pierce, with Dr. Turner and Ben!

Darius and Kenji made it to the platform as ravenous Dilophosaurs emerged from the trees. They stalked toward them, sensing Pierce's weakened state.

Kenji threw a shock orb at a Dilophosaurus. The thing hit the dinosaur, then rolled to the ground.

"They only work if the BRADs fire them," Darius realized. The Dilophosaurs snapped their jaws and came closer.

Suddenly, the snow glider appeared, flying right for them! The vehicle skidded to a halt in front of the platform, blocking Pierce from the Dilophosaurs. Sammy, Yasmina, and Brooklynn jumped out, making as much noise as possible.

Startled by the sounds, the Dilophosaurs backed off, slowly disappearing into the fog.

Brooklynn gave Kenji a hug, followed by a quick kiss on the cheek.

"How did you guys know we were here?" Kenji asked.

"What do you mean?" Brooklynn said. "You sent the BRAD-X to get us."

Darius and Kenji looked at each other, confused.

"No, we didn't," Kenji said.

Darius felt the ground fall out from beneath his feet. "It's a trap."

Red lights appeared through the fog as an army of BRADs marched in, surrounding the kids and Dr. Turner.

They watched as Kash stepped out from behind a BRAD, followed by the man who Darius heard back in the office. He wore a dark suit and looked at a tablet.

Ben recognized the tablet they had used to lure Kash to Dr. Turner's cave.

"You were right, Boss," Kash said. "Kid did have help."

"You all shouldn't leave important devices like these lying around," the man said. "They could fall into the wrong—"

As the man looked up from the tablet, he suddenly stopped speaking.

Kenji walked forward, his face losing its color.

"Dad?" he said.